"Back t

"I think so," Dana said.

"Good." Cal's answer had a determined undertone.

He scooped her up and laid her on the bed with an ease she found impressive. Still too relaxed to move, she watched as he picked up her dress and his shirt, then dropped them on the armchair.

When he was finished, Cal took his wallet and set it on the nightstand, then bent over her and divested her of her panties, garters and stockings in record time.

The mattress gave as he got onto the bed. He had her framed beneath him before she had time to blink.

"All rested up?"

Dana looked at him. "Um, I might need a minute or two more to recover."

He grinned. "Thirty seconds, then you're mine."

"I can be ready in ten," she offered after his first kiss. But she was lying. She was really ready in five....

Dear Reader,

Welcome back to Sandy Bend, Michigan, which you last visited with me in my February Duets novel *The Girl Least Likely To....* This time Dana Devine, best friend to Hallie Brewer, is seeking her bit of happiness.

The former town wild child, Dana has transformed herself into a savvy businesswoman. But just as she's about to open a day spa, her past comes back to haunt her. When her best friend's brother, sexy police chief Cal Brewer, is called to duty, Dana knows her heart is at risk. Can sizzling nights lead to love between a cop and a reformed bad girl? In quirky Sandy Bend, miracles have been known to happen....

I love hearing from readers! Stop by my Web site at www.dorienkelly.com, or send a letter to P.O. Box 767, Royal Oak, Michigan 48068-0767.

Happy reading!

Dorien Kelly

Books by Dorien Kelly

HARLEQUIN DUETS
86—DESIGNS ON JAKE
94—THE GIRL LEAST LIKELY TO...

THE GIRL MOST LIKELY TO...
Dorien Kelly

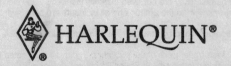

HARLEQUIN®

TORONTO • NEW YORK • LONDON
AMSTERDAM • PARIS • SYDNEY • HAMBURG
STOCKHOLM • ATHENS • TOKYO • MILAN • MADRID
PRAGUE • WARSAW • BUDAPEST • AUCKLAND

To Paulette for having the wisdom to celebrate her birthday in Chicago. To Sandy, Martha and Annie for the added inspiration (and the many martinis). And to Tesha, hairstylist extraordinaire.

ISBN 0-373-69122-X

THE GIRL MOST LIKELY TO...

Copyright © 2003 by Dorien Kelly.

1

DANA DEVINE didn't believe in revelations. That is, until her personal epiphany arrived in the form of carrot cake.

"Let me get this straight," she said to her best friend, Hallie Whitman. "You think this cake I whipped up is better than sex?"

Hallie set down her fork and subtly pushed her slice toward the center of Dana's kitchen table. "Maybe just the cream cheese frosting..."

Dana drew a deep breath. With luck, the mingled scents of cinnamon and freshly brewed coffee would have a sedative effect. Otherwise, someone was going to have to die.

Hallie had activities other than baking to fire up her nights. Dana, however, had occupied herself most of the past year with the quest for the perfect chocolate chip cookie. Recently, she had moved on to cakes. She had never imagined the day would come when thoughts of rich, dark chocolate and lighter-than-air angel food cake would make her feel sick and lonely, but there you had it.

"I know this is going to be a stretch for you, with your blissful newlywed attitude, but pretend you can bake yourself a big, fat carrot cake any night of the week. Now imagine you haven't had sex in, say... almost a year."

"Oh, Dana..."

"Let's up the ante," Dana said, flicking the edge of her plate with one fingernail. "Now I'm talking devil's food cake. And frosting made with the best Swiss cocoa I can get my hands on. What then? Would you take the cake or the sex?"

"I'm dead no matter how I answer this, aren't I?"

Dana sighed and absently ran her fingers through her short blond hair. "It's not like you can help it. After all, you married the guy of your dreams. But you know it's tough on those of us with a choice between carrot cake and...carrot cake. It's been six months today since my divorce was final and—and—"

Dammit! She was crying. Dana detested feeling sorry for herself. It wasn't as though she missed her ex-husband, Mike. After all, it was tough to miss a guy who'd been unfaithful before he had to decide on that traditional paper first-anniversary gift. Dana had presented him with some paper of his own—a divorce complaint.

Hallie pushed away from the table and retrieved a box of tissues from the counter. She handed one to Dana. "Are you okay?"

Dana wiped her eyes then rid herself of the tissue as if it were a smoking gun. "I'm fine. Really." At her friend's disbelieving scoff, she added, "I guess I'm a little tired."

Hallie accepted that, at least. "No shock, with the hours you've been keeping lately."

Life in their hometown of Sandy Bend, Michigan,

generally made for a skewed existence of empty winters and wild summers. A sleepy town nestled between the Crystal River and the sugary dunes of Lake Michigan, Sandy Bend had been "discovered" by wealthy city-dwellers from Chicago seeking a more relaxed pace. Each summer, growing numbers of them packed the town. Enormous shoreline vacation homes were gradually replacing quaint cottages. Trendy boutiques occupied formerly vacant storefronts.

Some longtime residents resented the influx of both cash and trunk-slammers, as the weekend residents were called. Dana wasn't upset. She could sniff out an opportunity at fifty paces and design the perfect plan to seize it.

Dana was big on plans. After all, a girl needed to be prepared. Her current plan filled half a notebook and most of her waking thoughts. She'd been working at a frantic rate to expand her hair salon into a full-service day spa to cater to the summer population. It was only late February, but already she felt as though she were running out of time. Dana said as much to Hallie.

"What's the point of having the day spa done if you're too exhausted to run it?" Hallie asked before digging into that cake she found better than sex.

Dana moved her piece aside. She wasn't very hungry, at least not for cake. "Tell you what, I'll be my own first customer."

"Very funny."

Seeking neutral ground, Dana asked Hallie for more detail on the mural she was planning for the Eden Room, one of several private spa rooms Dana was adding to Devine Secrets. It wasn't as though she was really worried about the design; Hallie was a fabulous artist.

As her pal moved on to other topics, Dana lapsed into silence and served up another slice of cake. She was feeling pretty absurd for letting loose on Hallie about Mike. While Hallie wasn't directly involved, she wasn't a disinterested party, either. Back in high school, Hallie had been Mike's date for the senior class bonfire. It had been a one-time thing—Hallie had been trying to get over a crush on wealthy and older Steve Whitman, who was now her husband. Mike was being a total ass, and trying to prove to Dana, whom he had a thing for, that she wasn't the only girl he could get.

Dana had taken the bait, just as he'd planned. One thing had led to another, and Hallie had stumbled on the two of them in the midst of a fully naked "apology" session in the back of Mike's car. Hallie had treated them to a beer bath, then escaped.

Dana had carried a case of the guilts over the incident until this past summer, when Hallie had returned to Sandy Bend after several years away. Hallie and Steve Whitman had fallen in love, and Dana and Hallie had made their peace and become true friends. Theirs was Sandy Bend's most unlikely friendship, which made Dana cherish Hallie all the more.

Hallie pointed her fork at Dana. "You're not listening to a word I'm saying."

Dana winced. "Guilty as charged."

"I was saying that you need to focus on something other than work for a while." With only the shortest pause, she added, "Have I mentioned that Cal broke up with Linda Curry last week?"

"Several times." Cal was Hallie's older brother, and somewhere along the line, Hallie had decided that her purpose in life was to nudge Dana in Cal's direction. Dana was pretty sure her purpose in life was to steer clear of Cal Brewer. Being around him made her crazy—and not a good kind of crazy, either.

"You know, I'm sure all you two need is—"

Dana reached across the table and hijacked Hallie's carrot cake.

"Hey, give that back!" Hallie made a grab, but Dana was too quick.

"No way. You can have it when you agree to stop talking about Cal."

The mutinous set of Hallie's jaw battled with her yearning expression as she eyed the carrot cake.

"Fine, no more Cal," she finally agreed.

Dana slid the cake halfway back. "Promise?"

Hallie seized her plate. "At least until the cake's gone, I promise. Here's a non-Cal question for you.... When was the last time you got away?"

It was one thing for Dana to dwell on the rotten state of her life. It was another to admit to it aloud. "Counting the hair show in New York?"

"The one last fall where you got food poisoning and didn't make it out of your hotel room? No dice."

"Okay, not counting New York, it was when I went Christmas shopping in Grand Rapids."

"A couple of hours down the road to shop isn't much of a vacation, but it's better than nothing."

Dana couldn't help the smug smile working its way across her face.

Hallie's eyes narrowed. "Wait a minute...Christmas which year?"

She knew she was beat. Dana leaned back until her head touched the top of her oak ladder-back chair. "Never mind," she said, staring at the arched pattern on the pressed-tin ceiling.

Hallie stood and starting pacing the small but nicely updated kitchen, one modern marvel in the middle of an otherwise thoroughly Victorian house. Dana sat up and followed her with her eyes.

"You've done wonderful things with Devine Secrets," her friend said, "but it's making a mess of you. Have you looked in the mirror lately?"

Dana snorted. "It's kind of tough to miss a mirror in my line of work."

"No, I mean have you looked at *you*, not your clients? You've got shadows under your eyes that even Trish, your cosmetics queen, couldn't cover, and I haven't seen you do anything new with your hair in months."

"I've been meaning to get around to it." Except she hadn't, really. She wasn't taking an interest in her appearance, which was a pretty scary concept for a woman whose looks and behavior were crucial to her business's success.

Lately, she'd had the bleak feeling that nothing mattered. No matter how sophisticated she looked or how hard she worked, a certain Sandy Bend faction was always going to view her as the wild thing she'd been in high school. And—to be honest—for more than a few years thereafter.

Hallie cut into her thoughts. "How about a sanity break, just for a couple of days?"

"And who will mind the shop?" The upside of having no partners was there was no one to second-guess her decisions. The downside was being held hostage to her ambition.

"You're closed Sunday and Monday. Shift your Saturday appointments and ignore the renovations."

The drab, blue-suited businesswoman who'd taken up residence in Dana's conscience barked, *"Certainly not! You have obligations!"*

Dana told her to clam up. Hallie was right; this was a matter of sanity. After all, she'd just lost it over a piece of carrot cake.

"So, hypothetically speaking, where would I go?"

A smile spread across her friend's expressive features. "We'll go to Chicago."

"Chicago." Dana sighed the word, making it sound like the paradise it was. She'd moved there after high school graduation, attended beauty school and then talked her way into a position as an assistant at a trendy salon just off Oak Street. She'd always had talent, and eventually that talent had earned her a chair of her own. She'd hooked up with a group of people who lived for the city's nightlife. Mike, who'd moved up in the ranks from a frequent fling to a sometimes-boyfriend, had come down from Sandy Bend almost every weekend. Life had been fast, hot and perfect.

While Dana daydreamed, Hallie apparently endeavored to push all the right buttons. Dana tuned back in just in time to hear, "We'll window-shop for shoes along Michigan Avenue...."

Shoes were Dana's one remaining indulgence—the sexier, the better. Deep discounts didn't hurt, either. Slowly, the rest of what Hallie had said sunk in. "Did you say *we?*"

"Sure! I could use a break, too. I mean, I love Sandy Bend, but sometimes it's easier to appreciate it after a couple of days away. A girls' weekend sounds great."

It did, but the reality of Dana's finances was a downer. "Except I have no money to spare and no place to stay."

Hallie smiled. "Easy. We'll drive together. You cover your meals and I'll take care of the hotel room. We can stay at the Almont."

"Yeah, right." That was like saying they'd bunk with the queen if they were in London. The Almont was a four-star hotel not far from the exclusive area where Dana used to work. "Are we going to rob a bank first?"

"No, really. Steve's family owns it, and I can guarantee we'll get a good deal, as in free."

To own an entire hotel was unthinkable to Dana, whose dad had run the local marina until he passed away when she was twelve, and whose mother spent her time pretending she was a yacht-owner instead of a yacht-tender.

"A free room at the Almont?" she repeated.

Hallie laughed. "Winter in Chicago isn't quite the same as springtime in Paris. Unless they're booked because of convention overflow—which I doubt—there are always open rooms this time of year. I'll talk to Steve, and we'll be fine."

"Speaking of Steve, how's he going to feel about you taking off like this?"

"No problem," Hallie said with breezy confidence. "It'll just give him a few days to miss me."

HALLIE'S STATEMENT about Steve proved to fall under the category of Famous Last Words. When Dana and Hallie checked in at the Almont's mahogany-and-marble counter Friday evening, a message already waited. While they were on the road, Steve had blown out his knee in a pickup basketball game.

Dana was resigned to driving the three-and-a-half hours back to Sandy Bend, but Hallie wouldn't hear of it. Instead, she arranged for a ride with her in-laws, who were heading to their weekend home on Lake Michigan. Dana could drive Hallie's car back on Sunday night.

Yes, Hallie had made it all sound so reasonable. It wasn't until Dana stood alone in a posh hotel room with carpet so deep it trapped her stiletto heels, that she realized she had no clue what to do with herself. Calling her old friends sounded more like punishment than pleasure. She couldn't afford to keep up with them, and didn't want to anyhow.

So what then? A night watching pay-per-view movies and scarfing down macadamia nuts from the honor bar?

"Totally pathetic," she told herself as she gazed out the fifteenth-story window. Below her waited a city offering everything an imaginative woman could envision from opera to nude steam baths rich with the scent and sting of a eucalyptus massage. Dana yanked the drapes shut as though she were closing out temptation.

She sat on the ivory brocade comforter and wriggled

out of her tall, black, man-eater boots. The boots lay on the floor pigeon-toed and unfulfilled. Like her, except the pigeon-toed part. She considered flopping back on the bed and giving up, but unzipped her overnight bag instead. Dana scowled at its wrinkled contents. She shouldn't have let Mike take their good luggage set.

He'd be doing more traveling than she would, he'd said—a reference to the wealthy girlfriend he'd found more useful than the wife he'd charmed and dazzled into marriage. She knew now that all Mike had ever wanted was a free ride.

Although it said little about her ability to forgive, Dana still felt a certain satisfaction that the wealthy girlfriend had dumped him within hours of the divorce becoming final. That luggage set was gathering dust, and Mike was wifeless, girlfriendless and penniless.

It seemed the penniless part bothered him most, not that he planned to do anything as rash as find a real, paying job. Sometimes Dana felt as though she'd aged to eighty, while Mike partied hearty in Peter Pan Land. Just last night, they'd had another argument when he'd arrived at the salon to ask for a loan. That he'd even consider asking her for money would be laughable if it weren't also telling evidence of the way she used to let him manipulate her.

Sliding open the mirrored closet door, Dana hung up the trim black pants and sweater she'd brought to wear window-shopping. She moved on to the vintage, tight-as-sin emerald-green dress—with matching pumps—she'd brought in hopes of improving her attitude toward men. Fat lot of good shoes and a dress would do if she succumbed to the lure of the television.

Before inertia seized her, she decided she'd have a shower, then take a trip downstairs for some music. When they were checking in, she'd seen a placard advertising a jazz trio in the bar.

On a whim, she carried the vintage dress into the bathroom and hung it on the back of the door so the steam could release the fabric's wrinkles. If she was going to work up the energy for adventure, she might as well be dressed for it.

Dana stripped in front of the mirror and, instead of taking an "I don't wanna look" glance she'd become so good at, forced herself to really examine her appearance. The shadows under her eyes were there, just as Hallie had said. She turned sideways and found reason to smile. It appeared that her recent hard work had rid her of the five extra pounds she always carried.

Was this a body she'd willingly show to a man? That is, assuming she could find someone back home who was willing to engage in a little discreet "no-lasting-commitment-required" sex.

Dana grinned at the thought. She was willing to bet that her breasts and bottom would be traveling south with gravity by the time she got lucky. Between her campaign to show Sandy Bend she'd become a reformed businesswoman and the way Mike had taken to shadowing her, the level of discretion she required didn't exist in her hometown.

She turned the shower's lever and gave a delighted laugh at the jets of water that shot from multiple nozzles on the tiled wall. When the shower reached the proper temperature, Dana stepped inside and closed the glass door. The water massaged between her shoulders and across her back. For the first time in months, her stress eased. She tipped back her head so the jets could spray her scalp. Maybe this wasn't better than sex, but it was a damn sight closer than carrot cake.

CAL BREWER loosened his tie and stepped into the bar at the Almont Hotel. Too tired to do much more than locate an open bar stool, he settled in. He'd just finished three hours standing in for his dad at a retirement party rife with cigar smoke and bad jokes. Since he'd also recently taken over his dad's role as police chief of Sandy Bend—well, interim police chief, in Cal's case—he was beginning to feel as though he'd stepped into someone else's life. Someone thirty years older who wasn't having a helluva lot of fun.

Right now it was a close call which Cal wanted more—a cold beer or ten hours of sleep. He'd been working gruesomely long hours and coping with a lot of political BS back home. He figured what the beer didn't cure, the sleep would.

While waiting for the bartender to finish up with a customer, Cal angled his bar stool so he wasn't facing an endless array of expensive liquors and took a quick glance around. The bar and the twenty or so tables in the lounge area were full. In a large, windowed alcove overlooking the city, a band played jazzy music. Not his usual style, but not half-bad, either.

The bartender, a slender redheaded woman in a white tuxedo shirt and black vest, settled a small bowl of salted nuts in front of him.

Cal smiled. "Dinner."

"And would you like a drink with your meal?" she asked. She arched her brows and broadened her smile as she checked him out.

"Whatever kind of Goose Island you have on tap," he said, referring to one of the local brews.

The bartender got down to business, and Cal leaned back and relaxed. He was glad he'd taken up Steve and Hallie on their offer of a hotel room for the night. Actually, it had been more Hallie than Steve who'd urged him to stay here. Cal had thought it was kind of weird of her to be so insistent, but, hey, this way he'd be fresh for the drive home tomorrow.

Besides, he'd always gotten a kick out of the Almont. Being here was like stepping into an old black-and-white movie. For years, this had been his and Steve's place to crash after partying their way down Rush Street. Not that Steve was a good candidate for a party weekend anymore.

It was still strange to think that his best friend had married his baby sister last summer, but they seemed happy. Actually, delirious was more like it. Cal was torn between embarrassment and a surprising jab of envy at how openly loving they were.

Envy didn't equate with wanting a wife of his own, though. He liked women too much to settle down. The real killer of the scrutiny he was subject to since his promotion was the way it had begun to affect his social life. The other candidate for police chief, a sanctimonious old goat named Richard MacNee, had cranked up Sandy Bend's gossip machine to full gear with references to Cal's alleged "dissolute lifestyle."

Dissolute, hell. He never dated more than one woman at a time and he never lied to any of them. Could he help it if he'd happened to date a lot of women over the years? He'd liked each and every one of them, and he suspected old Dick MacNee had never liked another human being—of either gender.

The MacNee and Brewer clans had never been friends. Years ago, when MacNee was serving a term as county sheriff, and Cal's dad was police chief, allegations of corruption had reached Cal's dad, who was ready to call in the state police to investigate. The phone call had never been made. MacNee had suddenly resigned and started a private security firm. His son, Richard Junior, now ran the family business, and MacNee seemed to be gunning for Cal. He didn't like it, but there was nothing much he could do besides protect his back.

With perfect timing, the bartender settled a frosty-sided stein in front of Cal. He nodded his thanks. The beer went down cold and easy as he marked time by the number of songs the band played. Two instrumentals later, he motioned for a refill. The beer seemed to be taking the edge off the tension that had been his constant shadow since stepping in as interim police chief.

The bartender settled mug number two in front of him. "Can I bring you anything else?"

There was nothing overt in her question, but the gleam in her eyes sent a different message. While Cal was appreciative, he wasn't interested.

"All set for now."

The only thing left on his wish list was that long

overdue sleep. His face hurt from the smile he'd kept plastered on during the party. He was lobbying hard to lose the word *interim* in front of "police chief," which meant being at his best even when he was over two hundred miles from home. The old boys' network ran deep in the law enforcement community. He always figured he'd have a few more years before his dad retired, but hell, this was his shot at being the big boss and he wasn't going to screw up. Cal hungered for this job. As a Brewer, police work was in his blood. He'd sacrifice just about anything to be chief.

Beer number three appeared after no more than a subtle lift of Cal's brow. He gave a passing thought to food. He'd skipped breakfast this morning. Lunch had been about two bites of cold, limp pasta at the retirement party, and dinner was the handful of salted nuts in their fancy silver bowl sitting in front of him. He should eat, but it would take too much effort.

As he drank, Cal eased into full relaxation mode. Yeah, he remembered this feeling and missed it, too. He knew that achieving it had more to do with being hundreds of miles away from Sandy Bend than it did with downing three beers. It still felt damned good. He intended to ride this wave until he crashed.

After another song, the band's vocalist announced they'd be taking a short break. The hum of conversation grew. It worked on Cal the same way the white noise inside airplanes did, making him feel disconnected from his surroundings. Then a new sound wrapped its way around him—feminine laughter so smooth and sultry that every man in the place who still possessed a pulse had to be sitting up and taking notice. Cal sure was.

A smile of anticipation and something not quite so friendly worked its way across his face. Now he understood why his sister had been so hot to see him settled at the Almont.

Cal knew that smoke-over-satin laughter. It was part of one sexy, smart-mouthed package named Dana Devine.

2

CAL PUSHED ASIDE his beer and again angled his stool toward the lounge. Twenty bucks said Dana was here with Hallie. And twenty more said they'd been waiting for him to show up. He checked out the tables for pairs of women, one blonde, the other sisterly and interfering, but no one suited the bill. Restlessly scanning the couples leaving the dance floor, he figured maybe Hallie had dragged Steve into her plot, but didn't see him either. He swiveled in the opposite direction to check the exit, and then turned to look at the dancers again. He'd just about decided he'd imagined Dana's laughter when he spotted her, then wondered how he could have missed her in the first place.

Her green dress was incredible—all about sex, yet without exposing much skin at all. Then there was the way she walked, as if she owned the place and was jazzed to have everybody at her party. He just might forgive Hallie for this stunt. In fact, in his current Zen-like state of contentment, thanking Hallie seemed a possibility. He'd never dated Dana, but for good or for bad, he'd always noticed her. Sandy Bend had its share of attractive women, but none so exotic, or with the potential to be as damned frustrating as Ms. Devine.

Cal stood without realizing he'd planned to. As he considered his next move—should he wait for her come to him?—a silver-haired man stepped even with Dana and she smiled at him. Cal's own smile wavered, then died.

Okay, maybe he'd gotten ahead of himself, figuring he'd been set up by Hallie. Or maybe it had been wishful thinking on his part. He scowled as he considered exactly what part had been doing the thinking. And how very many weeks he'd been ignoring that part.

Feeling like a kid who'd just had his favorite Christmas present taken away, he sat down and watched as Dana strolled from the dance floor. The guy she was with was old enough to be her father. Or grandfather. Except Cal knew this man was no blood relative. Not with that cocky male strut just because his hand rested at Dana's waist.

Definitely not grandpop having a friendly visit. So this was salon business, maybe? Cal's gaze narrowed as the man pulled out a seat for her at a round table where four other men already sat. Scratch business. None of them looked to be hair types—not that he'd ever seen hairstylists old enough to have tapped a pension fund dry. These guys looked plenty smooth, though. And plenty happy to have Dana Devine in their midst.

Curious, Cal leaned closer. He tried to catch their conversation, which was a colossally stupid move since they were twenty-five feet away. He couldn't hear anything but her laughter, a sound which wasn't helping his attitude. He'd never been able to make her laugh. Except maybe at him.

He turned to the bar and finished off his beer. The wise choice would be to pay his tab and pack it in for the night. The wise choice would be to ignore Dana, but he'd never been able to do that. Not since she'd returned to Sandy Bend married to Mike Henderson, the king of con men. And definitely not since she'd become single again.

Dana was eight years younger than he, the same age as his sister, Hallie. But unlike Hallie, Dana had never really been a kid. She'd always had an old soul, as though she'd experienced life before. She'd also had a quick wit and a knack for finding trouble.

By the time she was in high school, he'd been a member of the Sandy Bend police force—if six men could be considered a force. It hadn't taken Cal long to figure out that if he found Dana on a hot summer night, he'd also find a beach party, underage drinking and couples taking advantage of the privacy of the tall grass on the rise of the dunes. Funny thing was, he couldn't remember ever catching her with a drink or a guy. But she'd always been in the middle of the action.

He turned to watch her again. Tonight was no exception. Dana Devine was center stage and loving it. She wore a wide smile and her eyes sparkled with pure mischief. Her admirers laughed at something she said.

As he watched her, he tried to pin down the origin of the hot—almost impatient—anticipation coursing through him. Could it be he was feeling impulsive? Not possible. Good cops were never impulsive. Good cops were steady, reasoned thinkers. But right now he didn't have to be a cop, he reminded himself. He could be Citizen Cal, far from the snooping eyes of Sandy Bend.

A siren's lure, Dana's laughter drifted to him. A

dance and some conversation, he was sure that was all it would take to break free from this obsession. Tomorrow, he could tell himself that beer and tiredness had made him do what he was about to do. Tomorrow, he'd think about how totally wrong it was to give in to this craving for just a taste of her. He watched as the men raised their glasses in a toast to Dana, and she gracefully accepted. It galled him, the way she was oblivious to his presence, while all he could think of was her.

Cal signaled for his tab and settled up with the bartender, who did her best to ascertain whether he'd be back tomorrow night. At least someone appreciated him. That sense of underappreciation, of having been wronged in some mysterious way, impelled him toward Dana. The band was just returning for a set as he arrived at her table.

"CHECKING OUT THE BIG CITY?"

At the unexpected male voice, Dana—who'd been about to take another sip of the best apple martini in Chicago—slopped the chilly green liquid onto the tablecloth.

Her hand shaking, she set down the glass and glossed over her surprise with a composed facade. She scooted around in the leather club chair. Not that she had to turn to know who stood just over her left shoulder. Dana had known this man most of her life, fantasized about him naked for half of it, but had only managed to get along with him on the odd day or two.

The shock of seeing him was enough to make her

heart pound a wild beat. "Hello, Cal. You're look-ing—"

Downright edible, as always?

"—well," she said aloud. "What are you doing here?"

"Dance with me and we'll talk about it." He used the tone of voice she imagined he trotted out when he said, "Get in the back of the squad car."

Annoyed, she curved her lips into a sweet smile. "You make it sound so tempting."

"Dance with me...please." His facial expression was closer to a baring of the teeth than anything cordial. This, unfortunately, was the way most of their conversations went.

"Well, since you asked so nicely..." Gaze locked with his, Dana raised her fingertips to her mouth. Finger by finger, she flicked her tongue against the last sticky drops of apple martini. Cal's ice-blue eyes darkened. Not with desire, Dana was sure, but with plain, old-fashioned anger. She grinned.

Inclining her head to her new friends around the table, who were grinning themselves, she said, "Gentle-men, if you don't mind?"

They assured her they didn't, and she stood. She was no shrimp at five foot eight—plus a few inches of heels. Still, Cal seemed to loom over her. Dana edged past him and bought herself some breathing space.

"Ready?" he asked.

She nodded. Why did Cal Brewer always seem to sound annoyed when he spoke to her? She couldn't re-call doing anything especially rotten to him, except mock him when he'd been a rookie cop and she'd been walking adolescent attitude and Goth makeup. Maybe that was it, those months when she'd trailed after him as his own little shadow of doom in white face, midnight-purple hair and black lipstick. But that was years ago, and really, had been nothing more than a way to pass a boring Sandy Bend summer. He must be over it by now. She glanced up at his set jaw and impassive expression.

And they said women could hold a grudge.

When they reached the dance floor, Cal drew her easily into his grasp. For some reason, Dana's feet weren't working quite the way she intended them to. She stepped on his foot once, gave a hasty apology and tried to pay better attention to the music. Instead, her mind wandered to this T-shirt she'd seen in a gift shop back in Sandy Bend.

The shirt in question had read, One Martini, Two Martini, Three Martini...Floor.

At the time, she'd thought it was cute, but since she'd never tasted the drink, she hadn't fully appreciated the humor. Suffice it to say, with two-and-a-half cocktail glasses of the green apple variety warming her blood, the shirt's warning had taken on true depth of meaning. She felt loose-jointed and just the smallest bit reckless.

She'd never been this close to Cal. Even at Hallie and Steve's wedding, when Cal had been best man and she'd been maid of honor, she'd managed to escape to the bathroom immediately before they'd been called to dance together. Later, Hallie had accused her of being a chicken. Dana preferred to think of it as being skilled in self-preservation.

She'd been right to flee then and if she had any sense at all, she'd be running now. Cal made her too aware of the emptiness howling inside her. An emptiness that she suspected even five martinis couldn't numb. Cal's navy blue blazer felt smooth under her palm. Good quality wool, even if its conservative cut smacked a bit too much of Sandy Bend's Westshore Country Club for her taste.

She thought she caught the faint scent of cigar clinging to him. Like father, like son, she supposed. The closest Bud Brewer had come to running a nonsmoking police station was sticking his lit cigars into an ashtray in the bottom drawer of his desk. During her reckless days, she'd spent plenty of time on the opposite side of that desk receiving a lecture while watching grayish curls of smoke drift upward from the semiclosed drawer.

Like father, like son. That was another reason Cal rattled her. She wasn't the same girl who'd gotten into her share and someone else's of trouble, but she was still allergic to authority figures. Even those who were tall and muscled and could slow-dance their way into most women's hearts. Perhaps even hers.

Trying to distract herself, Dana hummed along to the pianist's ballad about lost opportunities and empty nights. Funny how the guy could make it sound so appealing, when the reality stank.

Cal cleared his throat, then spoke. "You've got an incredible voice."

"Thanks."

"Really sexy."

She smiled. "So I've been told."

After a moment, he added, "So, do you, ah, know those men you're sitting with?"

She shrugged. The motion was just enough to make her brush briefly against the hard wall of his chest. She pulled in a sharp breath and eased back a fraction. How could someone so emotionally distant create such a jolt?

"I know them now," she said. "They went to pharmacy school together in the early sixties, and have a re-union in Chicago each year."

He drew her closer. Dana knew she could wriggle away until there was once again a safe distance be-tween them. She also knew she lacked the willpower to do it. The heat this man threw off was better than that fantasy of a shower in her hotel room. Her eyes slipped closed as she allowed herself to think about Cal, herself and nothing but steamy mist between them. Her hun-ger grew as she imagined the feel of his broad hands sliding across her slick, wet skin to grip her bottom as he lifted her, and—

Bad thoughts.

Dangerous thoughts.

"Pharmacists?" he asked.

She blinked, trying to recall what they'd been talking about, then picked up the conversation just in time to avoid looking like a total idiot. "Yeah, they're phar-macists. Is that a problem? Do you think they're going to slip something in my martini and kidnap me into a life of bondage?"

"Doubt it." It sounded to Dana as though he half wished they would. She was half wishing herself away from here, too. The images playing in her mind were the sort that could get her into major hot water. Or a shower for two, if she was very, very lucky.

Dana shook off the thought. She began a mental litany of the reasons Cal Brewer was not a candidate for casual sex:

He was a cop, and on sheer principle, she was opposed to having sex with a cop.

He was her best friend's brother.

He was...

He was...sliding his hand down until it rested at the small of her back. Just the tiniest bit lower...

The pressure from his fingertips increased infinitesimally. Her gaze shot to his. His expression was relaxed, almost bland. She frowned. Maybe she'd just wished that whisper of a caress into being, but she didn't think so.

They danced in silence. Dana had never been more conscious of every inch of her skin, the way the satin of her dress rubbed against it, the heat of his body against hers and the answering fire burning where there'd been nothing but emptiness a few minutes earlier. She worked hard not to blurt an offer she knew she'd eventually regret.

Oh, the way this man could move, though.

"Are you in town alone?"

She not only heard the question, the sound of his voice vibrated through her. She was so close—too close—to telling him how very tired she was of being alone.

Not that Cal would care, or understand. Alone wasn't part of his vocabulary. He'd dated just about every available woman in Sandy Bend. Except her.

"Yes."

"Were you planning on meeting anyone?"

She leaned back until her eyes met his. His expression was guarded, as always.

"What's with the inquisition?"

He shrugged. "Just curious about what you're doing here."

Curious, she understood. Curious about how hot his mouth would feel against hers. Curious about how he'd react if she invited him up to her room for a night of no-holds-barred lovemaking.

It had to be the martinis sending her imagination where it had no right to be, but whatever the cause, she needed to escape. Dana gave him the type of response she would have given his father.

"I think the answer's pretty obvious. I'm in training to become a trophy wife. Tonight, dancing at the Almont. Tomorrow I go to Tiffany's and learn to spot a flawless diamond."

His mouth quirked, but it wasn't a real smile. "Are you always so sarcastic?"

Only when cornered, and being this close to Cal was like giving up her free will. She tried to tug away. "I should have stuck with the pay-per-view movies and macadamia nuts."

He held fast. "What?"

"Never mind." She wrenched free. "Look, this has been great and all, but I'm really tired and I need to get back to my room."

Silent, he walked her to the edge of the dance floor. As soon as she could, Dana shot away from him. She made her apologies to her pharmacist friends, picked up her purse and hightailed it toward the elevators.

As she did, she gave herself a pat on the back. Burning off sexual energy with Cal Brewer would have been about as bright as playing with explosives.

So why did she feel so miserable?

Her steps slowed. She took her time planting one green sling-back pump after the other on the ivy pattern trailing down the plush carpet. The unfortunate truth was she'd always been a woman with a fondness for fireworks, and had the scorched ego to prove it. This time, though, she'd played it safe. And while her move had been good and smart, safe was also as boring as her high school Citizenship class.

"Dana—"

Cal had followed her. Alarm—and something hungrier—tingled through her.

She picked up her pace, bypassed the elevators and headed straight for sanctuary, complete with its shiny brass sign reading Ladies' Lounge.

She didn't relax until the door closed behind her.

"Gotcha, Brewer," she murmured as she sunk into a cushioned floral-chintz armchair.

The door opened and Cal stepped in.

"You're kidding," she said.

He ignored her long enough to check out the stalls in the adjoining room for occupants. He emerged, apparently satisfied they were alone.

"Nice digs you women have," he said as he scoped out the mirrored makeup table with its bottles of perfume and hand lotion waiting on a lacquered tray.

She refused to meet his eyes, checking instead for

imaginary chips in her fingernail polish. "Not that it appears to give us any privacy."

He laughed as he settled on the couch that matched her armchair. "We're private enough."

"I was referring to women, not to the two of us."

"Want to tell me why you ditched me on the dance floor?"

"About as much as I want to be sitting in the ladies' room with a man."

"No, really," he said in a stony voice. "I'm not used to being treated like a plague carrier."

"This isn't about you."

His mouth quirked into a brief smile. "Really? I've always been pretty sure that it is. Anytime I get near you, I can practically see you sharpening your knives."

Dana shrugged, feigning a casualness she didn't feel. She didn't want to have a personal conversation with Cal. She didn't want that tempting sense of intimacy.

"That's your imagination," she said, not that she'd ever considered him an imaginative man. He was a cop, after all.

Cal stood. "Look, I don't figure we have much longer before someone walks in. I just wanted to apologize for asking you why you're in Chicago. It's none of my business and I know that. I got it into my head that somehow Hallie was involved, that she was trying to set me up again. She did everything but beg me to stay here tonight, and—"

Dana was a "big picture" kind of woman, and this one was arriving in screaming Technicolor. She had only the apple martinis to blame for not seeing it sooner.... Hallie Whitman was the Queen of Benevolent Schemers.

"I came here with your sister," she admitted. At Cal's self-satisfied expression, she added, "But you can spare me the end zone dance. If I had thought for a minute that she was trying to get us together, I would have planted my butt in Sandy Bend until it was old and arthritic."

He grinned. "Sandy Bend, or your butt?"

She rolled her eyes.

"So, where's Hal?" he asked.

"Steve blew out his knee. She had to go back home."

"Right. I'll believe it when I see him on crutches."

Dana stood and smoothed out the wrinkles in her dress. She noticed the way Cal's eyes followed her hands like a caress in their wake. The thought sent a warm, silken feeling curling through her.

"Do you really think Hallie would make up something like that?" she asked, her voice wavering.

"She's done more outrageous things."

Dana couldn't argue the point. "Apology accepted." She held out her hand. "Truce?"

His hand closed over hers. Once again, she could feel her will slipping away.

"How about a permanent end to the hostilities?"

"Fair enough." She withdrew her hand and walked to the door.

Cal pulled it open for her and ushered her through. "Evening, ladies," he said cheerfully to the matrons who'd been about to enter. Lips pinched tight with disapproval, they marched through the door he held for them.

"Have a good one," he added.

"I'm pretty sure they think we just did," Dana said as they walked toward the elevators.

He laughed. "And I'm pretty sure if we had, we wouldn't have been the first 'good one' that room has seen."

If we had... The possibility teased Dana, its image so real and tempting that she could think of nothing else.

They waited in silence until the elevator arrived. Almost unwillingly, she stepped in.

Cal joined her. He punched the button for the nineteenth floor, then gave her an inquiring look.

"Fifteen."

As the elevator rose silently and all too efficiently for Dana, he said, "I hope you have a great time tomorrow."

"Thanks. Are you sticking around town?"

"No, I'm leaving in the morning. I need to get up to my lodge."

Although spending the day with him hadn't been in her thoughts, disappointment washed through her. "Well, have a great time."

The elevator came to a stop and the doors opened. She pinned on a smile. "It's been...interesting."

He returned her smile, but then his expression grew serious. "The next time you see me in town, don't head the other way."

"I don't—"

"You do, but you don't have to." He leaned forward and brushed a lingering kiss against her cheek. Dana's willpower to step away had dwindled to nil.

She could do this.

She could ask him to her room, take care of the fire sparking between them, then forget about it tomorrow. She was sure she could do this.

Except she didn't have the guts.

She stepped through the opening. "Well, bye."

"See you around." The doors started sliding shut, the sound echoing that of her sinking heart. She had just thrown away the chance to live out a fantasy. Was she out of her skull?

She wheeled around and threw herself into the breach, forcing the doors open. "Wait!"

Cal arched his brows. "I'm waiting," he said as he settled one finger over the Open button on the control panel.

"I, ah...I was wondering if you'd like to come to my room for a drink." She pushed away the last of her doubts and worked up a little two-and-a-half martini courage. "Or something."

The elevator alarm started buzzing, but Cal just stood there, looking as casual as the night was long.

"Or something?"

She nodded. "Something."

Tilting his head to the side, he caught her in his gaze. "You sure about this?"

No, she wanted to blurt, *I'm not sure about anything except if I don't do this, I'll go crazy.*

"Positive," she squeaked, working past the lump in her throat.

The right corner of his mouth crooked up, as though he had spotted her bluff and was about to call it. He didn't, though. "Let me go up to my room for a minute."

Too dry-mouthed to speak again, she gave one last nod and stepped out of the opening. There, she'd done it—cast her fate, good or bad. Relief finally overriding nerves, she turned away.

"Dana?"

And back.

He was smiling, killer dimples showing to best advantage. "Your room number?"

Well, duh, as Amber, her favorite high school client, would say. "It's fifteen-twelve."

His smile grew even broader, and Dana found herself grinning in return.

"See you in a few minutes," he said.

There was a strong possibility she'd be dead of anticipation by then.

3

SANDY BEND was the Bermuda Triangle of cell phone operation. That, on top of the fact that Hallie usually neglected to turn on her phone, made for a shock when she answered Cal's call.

"So, is it his left knee again?" he asked, referring to Steve. "Or did you make the whole thing up?"

His sister didn't miss a beat. "Hello to you, too, Cal. And what kind of question was that?"

He smiled and sat on the edge of a bed he had no intention of sleeping in tonight. "A pretty good one, considering…"

She growled, as only his baby sister could. "It's Steve's right knee and he's here next to me in a lovely hospital gown. Bile green with black geometric print."

Cal heard Steve in the background announcing, "It's dog-ugly, and the television is broken."

Closer to the phone, Hallie was saying, "I'd let you talk to him, but he's filled with painkillers and likely to tell you all sorts of private things I'd rather you didn't know."

Cal grimaced. "The sentiment is mutual. Tell him I'll stop by on Monday, once he's home recuperating. And, Hallie, it didn't work."

"What didn't work?" she responded after a very telling pause. Good thing his sister had never decided to embark on a criminal career. He'd have had her tracked down and locked up inside a week.

"Setting me up with your pal Dana."

"You saw Dana? I had no idea—"

"Nice try. I saw her, we said hi and that was the end of it." His story was designed to protect the parties involved. Gossip hour at the Corner Café was a Sandy Bend tradition, and his legendary dating activities had already given the participants enough fodder without mixing in Dana's name. Talk about her wild years—the rowdy three a.m. Main Street revels and the outfits cut low enough to be illegal—had slipped into the realm of reminiscence not all that long ago. He felt this strange sense of protectiveness toward Dana, which was pretty dumb because he'd never met a woman more able to take care of herself.

His sister cleared her throat, evidently readying to work around his silence.

"Oh, well maybe—"

"Well maybe nothing." Cal combed his fingers through his hair, which was still wet from the shower he'd taken to lose the last remnants of cigar smoke. "I can find my own women."

She laughed. "That's never been up for debate. Whether you can stick with one of them for longer than a month is another issue."

"Butt out, Hal."

"I never admitted to butting in," she pointed out.

"No confession is necessary. I'm going by your prior record."

"What do you mean by that?"

He counted off the first three instances of meddling

that came to mind. "Think back to the couples' shower before your wedding, your wedding reception, your first day home after your honeymoon—"

His sister had the grace to laugh. "Okay, okay, I get the point."

"Take care of Steve, will you?"

"Of course, but if you happen to see Dana again—"

"Bye, Hal." Cal flipped his cell phone shut and grinned. Satisfied he'd thrown Hallie off track—for now, at least—he tucked his wallet and room card into his back pocket.

He took one last minute to ask himself if he knew what he was doing. He shrugged at the "probably not" that came in response. He wasn't sure what bizarre combination of fate and insanity had him hooking up with Dana Devine, but he planned to enjoy every minute. Never let it be said Cal Brewer didn't know paradise when he saw it.

WHEN DANA HEARD the knock on her door, she whirled from the bedside radio she'd just set to a jazz station. The pleasant martini buzz was beginning to fade a bit, but not enough that she was ready to chicken out.

"Coming," she called as she ran nervous fingers though hair she knew was beyond a quick fix. She'd already brushed her teeth and then gone through the "robe or dress" debate. "Dress" had won. No need to look as though she planned to immediately get naked, even though she did. Her nerves were too shot for delay.

Dana peered through the door's peephole. Cal had

obviously showered. His hair, still inky dark with dampness, broke into unruly waves. He'd also changed from his blazer and khakis into jeans and a casual shirt. She choked back a laugh at her initial thought that she was overdressed. After all, they both were for what they planned to do.

Knowing she couldn't stall any longer, she unchained the door and opened it.

"Hi," she said, motioning him in. Now that she was lacking the added advantage of high heels, he was taller than she'd thought. And she was more nervous.

"Hope I didn't take too long," he said as she closed the door and locked it once again.

"No...no, not too long at all," she stammered. "Can I get you a drink?"

Dana started fumbling her way through the small refrigerator with its elegant cherry-veneered door before Cal could answer. "It looks like I have...um, mineral water and imported beer and—" she should have checked before he came into the room and wiped out her ability to think "—and some white wine."

She wished there were more to dig through because she simply wasn't ready to face him.

"Dana?"

She eyed the jar of macadamia nuts. Technically, they didn't need to be chilled. The chocolate bar could probably live on its own, too.

"Are you planning on coming out of there anytime soon?"

Admitting defeat, she turned to face him.

He smiled. "That's better." Nudging her aside, he reached in and got himself a mineral water.

"How about you?" he asked.

"The same." She clasped her palms together and noted that they were the tiniest bit sweaty. Not good. While he set up the drinks, she walked to the window, pulled back the drapes and looked at the city lights.

He joined her. Dana took the offered water. Her hand trembled, but thankfully the chilly glass would take care of the perspiring palms thing.

He stepped closer to the window and looked up. "Good."

"Good, what?"

"I can see a little slice of the sky." He took a swallow of his water, then smiled. "I guess I have enough small-town guy in me that I need to see the stars—even when I'm in the city."

"Well, you don't get quite as many of them here."

"But the place has its compensations," he said, raising his glass in a toast to her.

Dana managed a lame, "Thanks." What had happened to that quick mouth she'd always taken for granted? "Would you like to sit down...or something?" She winced as the "or something" slipped from her lips. That phrase seemed to be launching itself with scary frequency tonight.

"Sure."

She watched as he glanced over his shoulder at the love seat, arranged to face the entertainment center that held the television and the honor bar.

"Hang on," he said as he stepped away and put down his glass.

Cal repositioned the small couch so that it faced the window. Apparently not quite satisfied, he switched on a bedside lamp at the far end of the room and then turned off the other lights.

"Better," he said, then picked up his mineral water from the now orphaned end table.

He sat. "Join me?"

Dana wasn't certain what she'd expected, but she knew this wasn't it. "Sure."

His long legs were stretched out before him. He looked every bit as relaxed as she was tense.

He reached his right arm over the side of the couch and set down his glass. Ah, now they were getting down to business. Now she could ease into the casual attitude she'd been trying to muster with her offers of cocktails and scattered conversation.

"You know," he said, "I've been doing some thinking about why it is you steamroller me every time we come near each other."

This didn't sound casual at all. Hoping to push past the topic, Dana worked up a breezy, "Have you?"

He nodded. "It's like the photo of you that hangs in your salon."

She didn't have to ask which one. He meant the black-and-white print from her early days here in Chicago. It was a seated nude, shot from behind. She was posed sitting next to a man as dark as she was pale. A narrow swath of black silk bound them together.

"You come at me the way you do for the same reason you chose that photo for your salon. It's like you're daring the rest of us to say a word."

She took a quick sip of her water. "The best defense is a good offense."

"You only need a defense if you're trying to protect yourself."

She answered without pausing to think. "Slick, Brewer, but I don't think you came down here for ten rounds of psychoanalysis."

"My point exactly. Do you think at least now, *here*—" he gestured at the intimacy of their setting "—you could relax a little?"

Feeling the need for distance, she began to rise, but he settled one broad hand on her bare upper arm.

"Okay, I'll stop." If she didn't know him for the love 'em and leave 'em guy he was, she'd think she saw regret in those usually unreadable eyes.

"Come here," he said. He drew her to him so her head was pillowed on his right shoulder. "Let's just kick back and enjoy the night—and the view."

Enough light shone in the room that their reflections—ephemeral yet riveting—shimmered on the glass in front of them. Dana lost all interest in the glittering lights beyond their paired image.

For a while, neither of them spoke. She learned the rise and fall of his chest, the beat of his heart, the clean, honest male scent that wrapped around her.

The longer she sat with him, the more her own heartbeat accelerated. She wanted something—anything—to happen. Yet, short of barking, "Would you mind moving it along?" she was fresh out of ideas to initiate the action.

Her seductress days were a distant memory. Besides, the thought of pulling an act on Cal didn't sit well. And that was all she feared her charm had ever amounted to—an act.

To distract herself, she asked, "So, just to even the score, what brought you to Chicago?"

He shifted a little and splayed his left hand over hers, where it rested against her thigh. Heat spiraled through her.

"Not good at peace and quiet, are you?" he said.

He didn't know the half of it.

"I came down for a retirement party. One of my dad's old buddies is retiring from the Chicago force. Dad's in Arizona, with no intention of coming back, so I represented the Brewers at the party." He paused. "I needed a break from Sandy Bend, anyway. It's not always an easy place to live."

"Especially with someone in the newspaper second-guessing your every move," Dana commented, referring to Cal's competition for the permanent job as police chief.

"Well, MacNee got on my nerves for a few weeks there, but I'm learning to live around him."

He wasn't enough of a politician to carry off his casual statement. She knew the sound of aggravation when she heard it.

She shifted her hand against his, so their fingers interwove. "MacNee's always been a pompous jerk. No one pays attention to him," she said, but they both knew she was skirting reality. Richard MacNee had set himself up as the all-knowing father of Sandy Bend. Nobody came across as more concerned, or as subtly condescending.

Cal sighed, a long-suffering sound, and brought their joined hands to his mouth to brush a kiss against her palm. "Why don't we leave Sandy Bend back in Sandy Bend?"

She relaxed. "Sounds good to me."

Jazz played low and soft in the background as they talked about Dana's favorite Chicago spots, and some of Cal's misadventures with Steve when they visited the city. After a while, conversation dwindled.

Eventually, Cal broke the silence. "I'm going to kiss you now."

She shifted to meet his gaze...and his kiss. She smiled at the humor curving his mouth upward. "Any reason you feel compelled to tell me first?"

"Just giving you a chance to say no."

"I was thinking more in terms of a yes."

"That's the best news I've had in a helluva long time."

He cupped her face with one hand. The kiss started warm and slow, not tentative. Dana already realized there was nothing tentative about Cal. Not the way he invaded the Ladies' Lounge. Not the way he said what was on his mind. Definitely not the way he kissed.

Soft and easy, possessive but not pushy, it was possibly the best kiss she'd ever had. Then again, it had been far too long since she'd had any man's mouth against hers.

Dana shifted impatiently and flicked the tip of her tongue against his upper lip. He took her act for the invitation that it was.

He tasted of minty toothpaste and hot male. She wanted to be closer, but the cut of her dress hampered her efforts. It seemed Cal could read minds, though, or at least interpret the frustrated groan that was as close to speech as she could come.

He reached behind her and slowly tugged down her zipper. Relief and anticipation overwhelmed her. Eyes closed, she leaned her forehead against his, as his fingertip traced the center of her back. When he'd gone as far as he could, she slipped from his grasp.

Dana stood and glanced over her shoulder at the open curtains. The building directly across from them was filled with offices, dark for the night. All other eyes were far enough away that she didn't care.

One Martini, Two Martini, Three Martini...Floor again drifted through her mind—a kind of insulation against exactly what she was doing.

She shrugged her way out of the dress's tight bodice and shivered at Cal's sound of approval as her breasts were bared to him. Her gaze locked with his, as she stepped out of the pool of sleek emerald satin at her feet. She had nothing left on but her black panties with matching lacy stockings and garters.

"Come here." His voice was low and raspy.

She shook her head. "Take off your shirt, first."

He didn't argue, didn't joke, just pulled off the shirt. He tossed it so that it landed on top of her dress.

Dana's mouth went dry. She supposed they'd been together on the beach at one point or another, but she had no recollection of seeing anything quite as magnificent as this display of muscle and breadth.

"Anything else?" he asked.

Much anything else and she'd be done for. She shook her head again.

He held out one hand to her. "Then come here."

She took the three steps that brought her into the vee of his legs. He ran his fingertips over the sensitive skin exposed between the bottoms of her panties and the tops of her stockings.

"I knew you'd be beautiful, but..."

She wove her fingers though his thick, damp hair as he traced the line of her waist. His hand moved higher to brush against the underside of first one breast, then the next. Dana drew in a shaky breath. She could feel a flush of color rising from her chest to warm her face. It wasn't embarrassment; it was hunger, hammering at her hard and fast.

She stepped out of his embrace, then knelt next to him on the small sofa. Bracing her hands on his shoulders, she straddled him.

She wasn't surprised that he knew what she wanted without her having to ask. With no prelude, no warning, his mouth closed over one nipple, already so sensitive that she cried out.

Afraid he'd think she felt pain, she managed a strained, "Don't stop."

"Wouldn't dream of it."

She'd been so starved for this she knew she was spinning close to the edge of release. Then, one arm still wrapped around her waist, he slipped his other hand beneath her panties and touched her where no man had in so long. Head tipped back in abandon, she accepted his deep and knowing caresses. She wanted to extend the pleasure, to revel in the sensation. Wanted to, but was losing her battle to retain control.

"It's okay," Cal whispered. "Go with it."

She had no choice, really; her body had decreed a rhythm of its own. All too soon, Dana arched and shattered.

SHE WASN'T SURE how long she'd been curled up, limp, damp and sated in Cal's arms, when he asked, "Back to earth now?"

"I think so."

"Good." His answer had a determined undertone.

After depositing her on the love seat, he stood, walked to the bed and peeled back the covers. Then Cal scooped her up and laid her on the bed with an ease she found impressive. Still too relaxed to move, she watched as he picked up her dress and his shirt, then dropped them on a brocade armchair.

He proceeded to strip with a single-mindedness that took her breath away. When he was done, he took his wallet and set it on the nightstand, then bent over her and divested her of her panties, garters and stockings in record time. He tossed them toward the armchair. About half of them made it.

The mattress gave as he got onto the bed. He had her framed beneath him before she had time to blink. When she did, her hands went above her head in total surrender.

"All rested up?"

She looked him up and down and knew her shock must be showing in her eyes. He was big pretty much everywhere. "Um, I might need a minute or two more to recover."

He grinned. "Thirty seconds, then you're mine."

"I can be ready in ten," she offered after his first kiss. But Dana was lying. She was really ready in five....

DANA SLEPT with a trust Cal suspected she never gave while awake. That made them a pair, he supposed.

She lay on her stomach, one arm curved above her head, the other tucked next to her so her hand rested beneath the pillow.

Careful not to wake her, he pulled himself up and leaned against the headboard. He gently rearranged the sheet until it rested just at the top of her thighs. The light shining in from the open curtains shadowed the curve of her bottom, the delicate run of her spine.

Cal thought again of the photo hanging in her salon. The few occasions he'd been in there had been sufficient to indelibly burn the picture into his memory.

Unable to help himself, he moved down to touch each distinct vertebra where it rested just beneath pale ivory skin. There was something so telling in this vulnerable bit of her, something he felt so connected to, though she wasn't his at all. And never would be.

With that thought, reality battered at the wall he'd built between them and the world. They were out there, just waiting for him—the guilt for having allowed himself this freedom, the regret that he couldn't have it again. He planned to fight off the inevitable until sunrise. Even longer, if possible.

He leaned forward and kissed the spot directly between Dana's shoulder blades, then moved down to her waist, and finally the base of her spine, just above the lush rise of her buttocks. She stirred, murmured something, then came fully awake.

She turned onto her back and gazed at him, but didn't say anything. He wanted to offer something, some words of how she touched him, but he'd never been very good at speaking his thoughts in a way women liked.

He saw the questions clouding her hazel eyes. Cal smoothed back a lock of blond hair from the smooth skin at her temple, then kissed her there, too.

She opened her arms to him, and he went willingly. This way, he could tell her. This way, she'd have to understand how incredible he found her. He knew she'd feel it.

THE CITY BELOW Dana and Cal woke and stretched. Buses growled their way down the street, and doormen whistled for cabs. Dana wanted to push back the day, but knew she couldn't. She shifted restlessly on the bed, then stilled, not wanting to wake Cal.

She studied him. He was beautiful, but in an entirely male way. The beginnings of a beard shadowed his face. Even with his summer tan faded, he had a golden cast to his skin, and a lean, hard strength that made her senses fly. He also possessed a tenderness she didn't dare think about.

Her marriage had left its mark. Any form of intimacy now made her freeze. She had screwed up big-time with Mike. In the midst of the leaving, the tears and accusations, she had sworn she wouldn't get emotionally involved with another man. She didn't have the time or heart left to give.

And even if she were in the market for something serious, she'd have to be crazy to think that Cal Brewer had any interest in her outside this one fiery encounter. Public officials tended to shy away from women with pasts like hers. Though it was just that—the past—she had too many secrets, too many wild nights, to be involved with Cal.

Richard MacNee would think he'd died and gone to hog heaven if he ever spotted her with Cal. She'd been Down 'n Dirty Dana ever since tenth grade. The name had been bestowed upon her by none other than Richard's son, who'd spread the rumor that he had sex with her under the bleachers at a basketball game. The only thing he'd ever gotten from Dana was a bloody nose for grabbing her. Still, who did everybody believe— Dickie Junior, the class suck-up, or Dana, the class rebel?

Feeling ancient, Dana slipped from the bed and headed to the shower. Soon, water pelted her and steam shrouded her. Being wrong was nothing new, except she couldn't recall the last time she'd been so totally, irretrievably wrong. Hands braced on the slate shower wall, head tipped down, she fought the frightened, sick feeling simmering inside. Why had she thought she was ready to emotionally disconnect from an act as intimate as sharing her body?

She needed to end this here, in Chicago. Today. Before she became tempted to beg for more.

Dana turned off the shower, stepped out and towelled herself off. She slipped into the robe she'd left hanging on the bathroom hook the evening before, pinned on a serene expression and padded back to the bedroom.

Cal still slept. She sat in the armchair not heaped with clothes and watched him, hoarding the sight. His eyes opened and his sharp blue gaze immediately found hers. It didn't surprise her that his innate wariness carried over into his sleep.

"Been awake long?"

She shook her head. "Just long enough for a quick shower." And some lengthy deliberations.

"I don't suppose I could persuade you to get back in bed?"

He could, but it would do neither of them any good.

She stood and glanced at the clock. "I thought you had to get back home. And I know I have some serious shopping to get done." She gave a pointed nod in the direction of his clothing.

His sleepy expression shifted into something harder. "So you're done with me? You're sending me out with the morning trash?"

Her attempt at a cheery laugh came off brittle. "Come on, Cal, don't get sulky. We both know the score. I'm in no more of a position to be continuing this...well, whatever this was, than you are. In fact, I'm not expecting so much as an invitation to coffee once we're back home. We might have left Sandy Bend for a while, but now it's time to accept reality."

He sat up and swung his long, muscled legs over the side of the bed.

Even now, when she knew she had to get him out of her room while she still had the strength, she took an instant to appreciate just how male he was.

And how angry.

He stood. "So I was what—a way of blowing off a little steam?"

She wrapped her arms around her midsection, trying to hold in the hurt. And the fear that Cal wasn't about to go peacefully. She'd had too many ugly scenes with Mike to be able to bear another one. She set her expression to match Cal's and walked away from the corner she didn't recall backing into. "I'm just saying what you're too polite to bring up."

At the look of surprise that crossed his face, she could tell she'd hit a direct blow.

He stalked to the armchair and began sorting his clothes from hers. "I get the distinct feeling I've been used for sex. And I gotta tell you, I'm not real happy about it."

"We were two consenting adults, who—"

"Save it. This consenting adult has never used a woman for sex. Never," he repeated in a flat and very hard voice.

"Oh, come on, with all the women you've dated—"

He raised the palm of one hand. "Don't argue this one with me. And don't come looking for a repeat performance. You're going to have to find somebody else to take care of your cravings. Got it?"

He tugged on his briefs. "You know, I thought there was something special about you…that beneath the attitude, you were someone I'd like to get to know one day." He shook his head. "Guess I was wrong."

There was nothing she could say.

Dana went back to the window while he finished dressing. After he was gone, she permitted herself the luxury of a cry. So much for the joys of no-strings sex.

4

CAL WAS NORTH of Muskegon by the time he was through feeling furious and had worked his way down to generally ticked. A lake effect squall had blasted off Lake Michigan, and US-31 was thick with ugly gray slush. It wasn't too much for his Explorer to handle, but enough that it required a slow pace and his full attention. All in all, the bleak driving conditions suited his mood.

He liked to think of himself as a pretty reasonable guy, slow to anger, fair to all. Anyway, that's how he would have described himself until this morning, when he'd developed a hair-trigger temper. What disturbed him the most about the entire disaster with Dana was the fact that he wasn't relieved to have found an easy out. After all, he'd gotten exactly what he'd bargained for—an unforgettable night and no strings. Unexpectedly, he'd also found something more. At least he thought he had, right up until he'd been given a pat on the back for services rendered. Or more accurately, a shove out the door.

Cal checked his rearview mirror, then scowled. Behind him, a red pickup truck wove through traffic at a speed that would have been stupid on a good day.

"Slow down, buddy," he muttered.

The truck blew past him on his left. It was one of

those extended cab jobs and so new that it still had its paper temporary plate in the back window. No payload to give that big cargo bed stability, either. He winced as the truck fishtailed. Why did the guys with the biggest engines always believe they were exempt from the laws of physics? Cal moved a lane to his right just to be safe.

Avoiding Sandy Bend and heading up to his lodge was also a matter of playing it safe. Not that the rambling family farmhouse he shared with his absentee dad and brother, Mitch, was a bad place; it simply wasn't the proper locale to work his way out of a funk. He needed solitude.

Ahead on the road, the flash of something unusual caught Cal's attention. He spat a blunt word as the red truck swerved into the center barricade, bounced off it and began executing slow-motion doughnuts across the highway.

He drew in a breath and tried to relax. There was no avoiding impact, so Cal tried to reduce the damage by taking his foot off the accelerator. In the stomach-lurching moment before it was his turn to be nailed by the truck, Cal wondered when, exactly, his whole life had become a car wreck.

AT ABOUT SEVEN O'CLOCK on Saturday evening, Dana pulled into her snow-covered driveway. She was glad she'd waited for the roads in Michigan to clear before escaping Chicago, even if every additional minute in that hotel room had been hell. Trying to distract herself, she'd stared at CNN on the television for what seemed like ages. Even so, if asked, she'd be hard-pressed to recite a single bit of news. That is, other than the fact that her love life had tanked once again. She figured she'd eventually recover from the colossal mistake of sleeping with Cal Brewer, but not today.

Overnight bag in hand, Dana trudged up the steps to her front door. The porch's deep overhang had kept the doormat clean of all but a dusting of snow. She stamped off her feet and unlocked the door. A quick glance told her that her shiny brass mailbox was full to brimming.

"Catalogs, of course." She grabbed the bundle and wrestled with the door again.

Once inside, she plopped the mail on an end table in the living room. The stack slipped and slid, then landed on the carpet. She bypassed the mess, dropped her overnight bag next to the couch and headed to the answering machine. Its light flashed three times in rapid succession. Dana pushed the play button. Elbows propped on the kitchen counter and head in hands, she listened.

"Hey, it's Hallie. Give me a call as soon as you get home. I just wanted to know whether...um, just give me a call."

Dana winced. "No way, José." She waited for the next message.

"It's me again. You know, I wouldn't have done what I did unless I thought that sooner or later, you two were going to get together on your own. I was just trying to speed the process. Um, well, I guess that's it for now."

The *process*, as Hallie had put it, couldn't have gone any faster. In less than a day, an entire relationship—

the thrill of meeting, the rush of passion and the ugliness of breaking up—had been pulled into the vortex of a black hole.

Dana didn't blame Hallie at all. The situation was no one's fault but her own. Before she could sink too deeply into berating herself, the beep preceding the next message drew her attention.

"Miss Devine, this is Len Vandervoort," an ancient, gravelly sounding voice announced. "You got the Notice to Quit, right? I need to know when I can start moving back in and—"

Whatever else her landlord was saying was lost as Dana dashed into the living room. She sat cross-legged on the ivory carpet, surrounded by catalogs full of springtime pastel photos of flowers and vacation wear. Her hands shook as she sent the mail flying. Beneath the phone bill, she found what she was dreading—an envelope bearing her absentee landlord's Florida return address.

Inside was one of those fill-in-the blank legal forms. According to the blanks he'd completed, she had thirty days to find a new place to live.

"Oh, no." In her heart and mind, everything tangled into an awful mess. Dana felt as though the last thing she was certain of was being ripped away.

Even though she didn't own it, this was her first home. In Chicago, she and Mike had lived in the same flat she'd rented before they had married. Money had been tight, mainly because Mike couldn't stop spending it, so they'd had some roommates who always seemed to party. Once she and Mike had moved back to Sandy Bend, at least they'd had their own apartment. That is, until she'd caught him cheating and had packed her stuff and moved out.

Pierson House, with its three stories of fantasy gingerbread exterior and peeling paint, was hers. The rent was cheap, thanks to rumors it was haunted by Old Lady Pierson, who'd disappeared ninety years before. Dana just considered the occasional inexplicable footsteps as part of its character.

She'd stenciled the living room walls, stripped layers of wax off the old linoleum and made the place sing. Now she had to hand it back to a man who'd left it vacant a good two years before she'd rented it. A man who already had another perfectly good house in Florida. How greedy was that?

Dana lay on the floor, arms spread. She stared at the plaster ceiling, which she'd painted a shimmering butterscotch gold. She wasn't sure if what her landlord demanded was legal, and knew it would cost her more money to find out. She was already paying for her divorce on the installment plan, and that was small potatoes compared to her business loan for Devine Secrets. Her palms grew clammy every time she thought about that number. How much expense would fighting an eviction add?

The short answer was, more than she had.

She rolled to her side and curled up into a ball among the catalogs. Maybe she'd just lie there forever, her form of passive resistance. When Vandervoort came to town, he could drag her bones out. It would serve him right.

By EARLY SUNDAY MORNING, Cal felt like a hostage in his own house. He'd escaped the accident with no major damage, just a bump and a bent rim that left the Explorer undriveable until the repair shop in Muskegon opened. His brother, Mitch, had picked him up and given him plenty of grief once he was sure Cal was okay.

To Cal's mind, "okay" was a relative state. Discounting issues of the Dana Devine variety—which, granted, was like ignoring a tornado bearing down on him—he supposed he was doing as well as a guy without transportation could.

Last night, he'd pushed aside thoughts of Dana and the corresponding need to escape to his lodge just long enough to fall asleep. The urge had returned today with a vengeance. Travel coffee mug in hand, Cal stood in the middle of the family barn. The old wooden building held such rarities as the float his family entered in Sandy Bend's annual Summer Fun Parade. Until this past summer when his dad had taken off to see the world, it had also held his father's classic Corvette.

Cal's remaining choice of vehicles was a tight competition between ugly and hideous. First, there was the gray '84 Dodge Ram pickup, on which the most appealing feature was the duct tape holding the sagging headliner to the interior of the cab. The truck had seemed to go into some sort of decline since his dad had left. Then there was the International Harvester tractor of indeterminate vintage—a definite loser of an option with six inches of snow outside.

Cal climbed into the Dodge. The keys were in the ignition, where they'd been since summer. Amazingly, the engine turned over and sputtered to life on the first try. Cal retracted every cutting thought he'd had about the truck's appearance.

After checking some loose duct tape to make sure the headliner wouldn't become a shroud, he backed out of the barn. Once down the large earthen ramp and on level ground, he pulled the parking brake, climbed out and began to slide the barn door shut. His work was interrupted by a shrill whistle from the farmhouse porch.

Cal knew it was Mitch, so he didn't bother to turn. His brother wouldn't be hunting him down to tell him he'd won the lottery or they'd struck gold in Sandy Bend. No, Mitch was guaranteed to be on his tail for bad news. Work news, since Mitch was also on the Sandy Bend police force.

"Hey! Are you deaf?" his brother shouted.

Defeated, Cal turned to face him. "Whaddya want?" he yelled back.

"Rob Lorimer's wife is having her baby."

"And?" He'd no sooner prodded his brother than he recalled the answer to his own question. And it wasn't an answer he liked. He grumpily scuffed one work boot into a snowdrift.

"He says you're scheduled to cover for him."

Cal winced at hearing the words aloud.

Mitch closed in on him. "He needs you now. Something about Cassie's water breaking and other childbirth stuff I didn't want to hear. Bottom line...you promised."

Actually, Cal had earned that duty over a losing coin toss with the department's rookie member. He should have pulled rank, but that wasn't his style. So here he was, ten miles from his lodge and with no potential of getting any closer.

Cal parked the truck in the barn, then thought about closing himself in, too. Barring the door and hiding from the world didn't sound bad. In fact, his dad had installed inside door locks for that very reason. When one of the kids pulled a dumb stunt, after dispensing justice, his dad would go to the barn and tinker with his Corvette as a way of blowing off steam.

Just thinking of his dad made Cal smile. After his wife's death, Bud Brewer had single-handedly fed and raised his children. He'd loved their mother so completely that until very recently he'd fended off every question about remarriage. Though at present, Cal couldn't manage even some hot, Chicago fun, he wanted to love like that one day.

"Don't even think of closing yourself in there," Mitch called from just outside, breaking off Cal's thoughts. "I'm pretty sure I can make it through the window over the milking stall. Besides, I'm feeling generous—I'll even drive you to town."

Cal shook off the remainder of his black mood. It was a damn good thing he loved both his brother and his job.

SUNDAY MORNING had dawned clear, and Dana had been wide awake to witness it. During the hours when she should have been sleeping, she'd had fitful dreams that she hadn't really graduated from high school and she'd have to go back and take phys ed again. She knew it was just stress snaking its way into her subconscious, but that didn't make this morning's puffy eyes and foggy mind any easier to deal with.

While she drank her morning coffee, she'd considered calling Mr. Vandervoort and asking him if he'd postpone his move back to Sandy Bend. She'd eventually concluded there was no point in delaying the inevitable. Even a few months longer wouldn't change the fact that she was starting over. Again.

By seven o'clock she'd done ten or so of the one hundred abdominal crunches she knew she should be doing every day, had eaten a yogurt and a freezer-burned bagel, and had dressed in her grubbiest clothes. She was more than ready for some construction mayhem at Devine Secrets.

Luckily, she could take out her aggression on a wall she had to take down in what would eventually be Athena's Escape, a private massage room. Since Dana's grand plan didn't require a masseuse until June, a few hours with a sledgehammer would serve to alter her mood, which lingered somewhere south of cranky. She'd conjure Mr. Vandervoort's face—not that she'd ever seen him—then swing with all her might. It was cheaper than therapy.

As was her habit, Dana walked the five blocks from her home to the salon. Hands tucked into the pockets of her favorite winter parka and face tipped down to avoid the bite of the wind, she tried to list the good things in her life.

One—I have a best friend who would do about anything for me.

Maybe "*to* me" was more accurate, considering the way Hallie had set her up with Cal.

Two—I have my health.

Okay, so maybe she shouldn't examine that one too closely, either, given her sleep-deprived state. Or the fact that mental health fell under the same banner, and what she'd done with Cal was downright crazy.

Three—I have my business.

Dana smiled a smile of pure relief. The business part was true. She knew that being totally in love with her job was uncool, but she was the adult version of that kid back in high school who panted and drooled while volunteering to answer all of the teacher's questions. Of course, back then she'd been slumped in her seat doing her best to prove that she was different than Catherine and Josh, her two overachieving older siblings—a point she'd established vividly with Sandy Bend High's faculty.

As fate would have it, though, Dana was simply a late-blooming overachiever. She had turned around her life and seized success. Maybe even in her new, improved persona, she wasn't suited for country club men, as her nastier classmates had predicted. No matter what else happened, she could look at Devine Secrets and take pride in how far she'd come from being viewed as her high school incarnation of Down 'n Dirty Dana Devine, Sandy Bend's wild child.

She neared the salon with its flower-bordered sign hanging above the stairwell. Instead of taking the customer entrance, she walked down the sloped side street toward the back of the spa. At the bottom of the street was a small parklike area overlooking the currently frozen Crystal River. In the summertime, she planned to have a friend give yoga classes on the broad ribbon of grass. Hard to imagine now, with last night's snow covering the expanse.

Dana frowned as she glanced at the path in front of her. She wasn't the first person here. She knew that Missy Guyer, the insurance agent next door, wouldn't be working on a Sunday. Sandy Bend's former homecoming queen, class president and leader of the popular clique treated her business as an amusing hobby. Besides, the footprints were too large for perfectly petite Missy. In fact, there was too much variety for them to be just one person's.

Reaching deep into her jacket pocket, Dana grabbed her keys and quickened her pace. An ugly feeling had settled in the pit of her stomach.

The tracks led straight to the rear entry of Devine Secrets. And she wouldn't need her keys. The salon's back door stood wide open. A stream of water rushed out, adding to the treacherous blanket of ice that had already formed.

She told herself that any sane person would turn back and get help. However, she wasn't feeling particularly sane. Gripping the door frame for balance, she slogged through the mess, then headed to the storage room—the logical source of the flood.

"Dammit!"

Instead of a broken pipe, as she'd half-hoped, the spigot to the utility sink flowed full force. Water sheeted down the front and sides of the white plastic tub. She ignored the alarmed voice in her mind asking who could have done this, and focused on fixing the mess.

Dana turned off the tap. Not even bothering to remove her jacket, she reached into the icy cold water and pulled out a rag jammed tightly into the drain. With an angry cry, she flung the sodden mess to the floor.

Taking care not to slip, she returned to the open back entry. She supposed she should be grateful that the floors sloped to the rear of the old building, and not to the front. And she should be thankful that all the renovated rooms were safe from the flowing water. After kicking loose the ice that had built just over the threshold, she slammed the door.

"Okay," she said to herself, "we simply pick up and move on. That's what we do, all right." Her utter lack of conviction made her wonder if she shouldn't take a few cheerleading lessons from Missy. She also wondered who the "we" was she'd heard herself referring to. In truth, she'd never felt more alone.

Dana unzipped her soggy jacket and hung it on a hook in the utility room. *I'm trying to be positive,* she pointed out to whatever kind and guiding spirits were in charge of hairdressers who'd maxed out on stress. Just a little help would be nice....

She turned up the thermostat in the hallway. A few extra dollars on her heating bill were less worrisome than the chance that some of her hair-coloring products might be damaged by the low temperature in the salon.

The salon...

She glanced at the doorway that led to the finished part of her property. The part where some real damage could be done.

Her heart drummed a double-time beat. Operating

on sheer panic, she flew into the salon. She'd gone no more than two steps when her feet slid from beneath her and she landed hard on her tailbone and elbows. Pain shot up her back, taking with it the ability to draw a breath. She lay back and felt the slick, viscous liquid on the linoleum. She turned her palm over and looked at the stuff coating it. Shampoo and hair coloring.

Gasping for breath, she rolled to her hands and knees. How could she have missed the open tubes, packets and bottles littering the floor? Sobbing, Dana crawled back to the doorway. Still hurting too much to stand without help, and unwilling to spread the damage by touching the walls, she fought to catch her breath.

Mike. It had to be Mike, she thought, feeling almost disconnected from the chaos around her. Sabotaging her salon was so infantile and petty it had to be him.

Mike, whose idea of hiding the fact that he was sleeping with someone else, was to come home, take a shower, then dump all his clothes smelling of the other woman's perfume in the laundry pile.

Subtle was not his middle name.

Dana worked her way to her feet. She made her way back to the storage room at a pace even elderly Olivia Hawkins, one of her regular customers, could beat. It was as though the fall had knocked more than Dana's breath from her. It had taken her heart, too.

Once she stripped out of her dye-and-soap-covered jeans and shirt, she scrubbed her hands and face. Dana checked the bruises already blossoming on her elbows, then dressed in the spare change of clothes she always kept in the salon. Unfortunately, she hadn't gotten around to switching to winter wear, so she was stuck with a pair of white shorts and a skimpy black sleeveless top.

She hauled out the bucket and mop, plus all the rags she could get her hands on. She was about to start cleaning when those guiding spirits finally made their presence known. It struck her that she should call someone...maybe even the police. And before she mopped up the evidence, obviously.

"Dana Devine, world's densest victim," she muttered.

The phone was in the front of the salon, through the minefield of soap and rust brown, red and purple ooze. Dana kept to the perimeter, though it was still far from easy going. When she reached the phone, she lifted the handset and dialed 9-1-1. The woman on the other end got the facts from her and told her that someone was on the way.

Dana stood in the front room, looked at the way Mike had messed with her life once again, and felt the numbness that had taken over her soul give way to icy anger.

Ah, being mad felt good; being mad felt cleansing. Mike the weasel deserved to be in jail, and the sooner, the better.

COVERING FOR ROB meant at least Cal had a car. This was Cal's only uplifting thought as he drove the miles from his daily loop through Sandy Bend's countryside to the location of the call he'd just taken. A call that summoned him to the last place on earth he was prepared to be—up close and personal with Dana Devine.

He pulled in front of the salon, got out of the cruiser and reminded himself that he was a professional. Damn crying shame, too, he admitted as he made his way down the snow-covered steps to the basement entry of Dana's salon.

Cal looked at the frou-frou flowers on the entryway walls and winced. This place had suited Dana better when it had been the Hair Dungeon, before she and Hallie became joined at the hip, and his sister had painted all the girly flowers and ivy on the walls. Not that Dana wasn't feminine; she just wasn't flowery. She was more of a fire and seduction sort of woman. The kind that should scare the hair right off any reasonable man. Stupid him for not having been scared on Friday night. And even more stupid was his bizarre sense of anticipation—hunger, even—at the thought of seeing her again.

He tugged on the front door, but it was locked. Even though he could see Dana through the glass side panel, he pounded on the door's shiny, forest-green surface. It felt good to use up some of his frustration on the door, though he still had plenty to spare.

He looked through the side panel again and that incipient frustration grew. Why was she dressed for a summer picnic, with a couple of inches of skin exposed between the top and shorts? Skin that he knew all too well was hot and supple but had an alluringly innocent taste of peaches. He tried to focus his gaze elsewhere, but couldn't. Dana hadn't moved from her spot next to the reception desk.

"Would you let me in?" he called.

She shook her head emphatically no. "Go around."

"Just let me in."

"Too slick...go around back."

Slick? He'd been told he was dealing with a B and E. Shock rippled through him as he realized he still hadn't looked anywhere but at Dana. Years of training had been obliterated by the sight of one sexy blonde.

Muttering to himself about getting a grip and being a professional, Cal trudged up the front steps, around the corner and to the back door of the new space Hallie had told him Dana had rented.

He noted the glacier of ice that had built up just outside the entry. Strange. The door swung open. Dana stood on the other side.

He dragged his gaze past the hot little outfit to note that she was barefoot. In her left hand was a towel soggy with something that looked like muck and rust and even slimier stuff.

"How many people are in the police department?" she asked in a flat voice.

"Six."

"How about calling one of them?"

True, he'd rather be scrubbing the station floor with a toothbrush than be here, but it really bugged him to know he was unwelcome. Then again, what had he expected?

"This was my call. I took it and you're stuck with me. Now you want to tell me what's going on?"

"When I got here about half an hour ago, the back door was wide open and someone had flooded the place."

A mix of annoyance and alarm shot through him. He

couldn't believe what he was hearing. "So you just walked right in?"

"Trust me, the person who did this isn't the sticking-around type."

Better and better. "Just how do you know that?"

She motioned him into the building. As he followed her down a hallway with half-painted walls, she said over her shoulder, "Because Mike did it."

"Mike?"

They stepped through what was obviously a recently cut entry into her original salon space. "Henderson—my ex-husband? And no one is worse at sticking around than Mike."

Cal looked at the brownish liquid slowly seeping its way behind a short row of hair washing sinks. The place was a total mess. "Why do you say it was Mike?"

"We had a disagreement here in the salon before I left for Chi—" She stopped abruptly.

"Left for where?" he asked, still more focused on the evidence littering the place than what she was saying. This damage looked like the work of a pack of bored kids.

"For Chicago."

"Oh," he said, wishing he'd never asked. "Right."

They spent an uncomfortable moment, and he was no more willing to meet her eyes than she was his. His gaze wandered to a photo on the wall—the nude of Dana—then skittered away. He tried to think of something—anything—than the feel of her beneath him on Friday night. And early Saturday morning...

He swallowed hard and forced himself to look at her. This time, her eyes locked with his. Cal felt an unsettling sense of having been deprived of something special and rare. He reminded himself that their time at the Almont had been about nothing but sex, and that it was in the past. That was the way an almost police chief needed it to be, and Dana wanted it to be. So what if they had shared the most incredible sex he'd ever experienced? So what if he felt a reluctant attraction to this woman, though she didn't seem to feel even a sense of basic social politeness toward him? So damn what? Ah well, if nothing else, in Chicago he'd learned the price of throwing away caution.

"Aren't you going to take fingerprints or something?"

The tremor to her voice was so slight Cal thought he might have imagined it. Except she had her arms wrapped about her midsection, and she looked so lost that the sight was nearly enough to melt the ice he'd built around his heart.

"Mitch will be here in a few minutes," he said in his best "just the facts, ma'am" tone. He needed to keep a professional distance. "So, what was the disagreement about?"

She shrugged. "The usual. He wanted money. I didn't give him any, and he got even. Are you going to arrest him?" she more demanded than asked.

He fought back the smile he felt forming. He knew Dana well enough to be sure she'd remove it for him if he let it show. "If I went around arresting men on the basis of their ex-wives' claims, I'd have half of town in jail."

"So you're saying that I made this up? Or that I did this to frame him?"

"Look, just start at the beginning and tell me what you saw."

She recited her story with a clarity that left him impressed. He needed to ask for additional details only a few times. Then she finished up with, "It's Mike. I'd bet my last dollar. That is, if I didn't have to spend it to replace all of the hair products he destroyed."

Cal looked up from his notes. "Have you called your insurance agent?"

"I know better than to wake Missy Guyer before noon."

She had a good point. She was also on target in wondering about her ex. Still, even a town as small as Sandy Bend held its share of suspects.

"Is anyone else angry at you? Have you had to fire anyone lately? Or had any trouble with the guys doing the renovation work?"

"I haven't fired anyone, and when I can, I work right along with the guys, so we get along fine."

A woman who could swing a hammer *and* sing the blues as if she'd been born in the twenties instead of the seventies? The thought was downright mind-boggling.

She spurred him back to the matter at hand. "Cal, I'm telling you it was Mike."

"I appreciate the guidance, but let's not stop at Mike. How about any mishaps with a customer?"

He could almost see her hackles rise. "Mishaps? I'm a professional. Of course I've had customers who haven't been perfectly happy, at first. I've worked out ninety-nine percent of the problems, and the rest make a career of being dissatisfied." She shook her head.

"All of them would worry too much about chipping a nail to do this."

Okay... That narrowed down the field to what he suspected was going to be an even more sensitive subject. "Any men? Current boyfriends?"

"Men besides Mike?" she asked. She began to say something more, then stuttered to a stop. It was all Cal could do not to take a cautionary step backward as the full implication of what he'd asked began to register.

"Current boyfriends?" she echoed, her color rising in dangerous flags over her cheekbones. "Do you think that I'd have been with you in Chicago if I had a boyfriend?"

"I have to ask the question."

"So who do you think I'm dating? The town baseball team?" She stalked closer. "Here's a newsflash for you, Chief. There has been no man in my life since Mike and I split up. Not one in over a year. Except you, that is. Much as it kills me, I guess I'm going to have to count Friday night, aren't I?"

Cal could feel a muscle at his jaw twitch as he fought to keep his expression impassive. Her jab shouldn't hurt, but it did.

"I'm just doing my job," he replied, since any direct answer to her question would be the modern-day equivalent of impaling himself on his own sword.

"Yes, you're doing your job," she said, "with a total lack of tact and sensitivity. But since you've raised the question, let's play it out. You've slept with me, so that makes you a guy with a motive." With a sweep of her arm, she gestured around the salon. "Is this your payback, Cal? You left Chicago plenty mad."

Cal turned when he heard somebody behind him cough. Mitch stood framed in the entryway to the new spa area. "Ready when you are."

The gleam of interest in Mitch's eyes told Cal how long he'd been there. Cal ignored his brother and focused on Dana.

"Look, Dana, Mitch and I are going to take some photos. An investigator from the county sheriff's office should be here soon, too."

She threw up her hands. "Whatever," she said angrily and stalked down the hallway where Mitch still stood.

"So...you and Dana?" Mitch asked after Dana had disappeared.

"It's none of your business."

Mitch's answering grin ground on Cal's nerves. He could remember a day when he'd been as easygoing as Mitch. It hadn't been all that long ago, he supposed. Not that the past—including that night with Dana, which they clearly both regretted—mattered now.

"Get to work," he barked at his brother.

"Yes, sir," Mitch answered in a voice as dry as the dunes north of Sandy Bend.

Cal blew out a weary breath. He should have gone to his lodge. Or barred himself in the barn. And he never, ever should have given in to temptation with Dana Devine.

5

AT EIGHT-THIRTY Tuesday morning, Dana sat across the desk from Ted Hughes, Esq. Ted had handled the incorporation of her business and the dissolution of her marriage with finesse and a hefty bill. Whether he could keep a roof over her head remained to be seen.

She took a nervous swallow of her coffee and watched as Ted read through the notice Mr. Vandervoort had sent her. Watery gray daylight sifted through the office's front blinds.

"Give it to me straight," she asked when Ted was through reading. "Can he do this?"

Ted slid the papers back across the polished walnut desk. "You're the poster child for poor legal decisions, you know that?"

She'd known Ted forever, so she was willing to take a few blunt truths from him. "That bad, huh?"

He leaned back in his chair. "You never signed a lease, Dana. If you had, we'd have some basis to fight him. But as it stands, you pay your rent monthly, so all he needs to give you is one month's notice."

"Any good news?"

Her lawyer grinned. "I won't bill you for the bad news."

It could be worse, Dana thought, then gave a wry shake of her head. The way things were going, she might as well have that chiseled on her tombstone: It Could Be Worse.

She stood and extended her hand. "You're the best, Ted. I appreciate the break."

She was no sooner back on the sidewalk than her "it could be worse" philosophy was put to the supreme test. Mike, her ex, lurked at the corner. Dana debated turning back and taking the long way to the salon, but refused to give Mike that kind of power over her.

"Neither rain, nor sleet, nor gloom of night, huh?" she said as he approached.

He looked skyward, then gave her his patented charming smile. "What do you mean? It's daytime."

"Never mind."

He settled a hand on her arm. Dana drew away. She looked at him with as much objectivity as she could muster. Mike was a handsome guy, in a slick sort of way. He was tall with perfectly cut golden hair, and teeth he'd—well, actually *she'd*—paid a ton of money to get veneered to a blinding Hollywood white. The money was supposed to have been a loan. After that, she'd learned to be a lot more specific about the terms of repayment.

Still, she could see why she'd fallen so hard for him, and why other women did with such nauseating frequency. But on a subjective level, she knew that if the Almighty had equipped Mike as He should have, the man would have a forked tongue and scales, because he was a big-time belly-crawler.

"What do you want, Mike?"

"Why should I want anything? Can't a guy be concerned about his ex-wife?"

She supposed some guy, somewhere, might be. But Mike? "Why start now?"

"Dana, I hate to see you this bitter. I was just wondering why you were visiting Ted. Is it the trouble you had at the salon?"

"How would you know about that?"

She noted the way his eyes flickered away from hers before he said, "Around here, all it takes is stopping for a cup of coffee."

A point she'd have to concede, especially since more than one concerned citizen had pressed his nose to the front door of the salon yesterday, when she'd been scrubbing and bleaching, then scrubbing some more. She'd ignored everyone, as well as the persistent ringing of the telephone, preferring to suffer alone.

"So, come on, what's up with the visit to Ted?" Mike prodded. "Anything I can do to help? I warned you it was going to be tough going into business on your own."

Yes, he'd warned her when he'd asked for a share of the salon...not that he was willing to put up any cash for his percentage. He just figured he was owed it because he'd "given her a start," as he'd put it. The truth was a whole lot uglier. Dana couldn't stop the rush of anger bearing down on her.

"You want to help me? Like you did when you cheated on me with Suzanne Costanza, whose best asset is her bank balance? Or maybe like the time you cleared out my savings so we had to move back from Chicago in the first place? You've helped me enough, thanks."

He rambled on in his salesman's patter, as if she

hadn't spoken. "Let me buy you breakfast—scrambled eggs and hash browns, your favorites. I've got a new deal in the works, and I want to tell you about it. I think it could be a big break for us."

He lifted his hand to her face. She knew he was going to run his finger down the bridge of her nose as he used to. Once, she'd found the gesture endearing. No more, though. She wrapped her fingers around his wrist in a no-nonsense grip.

"Don't you get it? There is no *us*. We're divorced. Whatever new deal you have cooking doesn't interest me. You're no more a part of my life than that lamp-post over there. Now, I'm having a really crummy day, and if you want to survive with your liver intact, you'd better cross to the other side of the street." She released his hand.

He patted the top of her head. "That PMS is still getting you down, huh?"

If she followed through on her threat of liver removal, would the act be considered justifiable homicide? Regrettably, Dana had her doubts. Still, she'd get the cheap thrill of having Cal frisk her before she began her life behind bars. The thought held a certain twisted appeal.

Based on the way Mike's eyes widened as he took in her expression, he must have realized his liver was in true peril. He checked his watch. "Gotta run."

If she weren't wearing suede snow boots that actually hated snow, Dana would have seen just how fast she could make Mike sprint. As he hustled in the opposite direction, she picked up her pace to Devine Secrets.

"It could be worse," she murmured. This time, she could almost see some truth in the statement. She could still be married to Mike.

The closer Dana got to the salon, the more her optimism kicked into gear. Each Tuesday—the start of her workweek—was the beginning of something fresh and exciting. On a Tuesday, she could even face a visit by Cal Brewer.

By the time Dana reached the back door of the salon, Trish, her facial and cosmetics expert, stood outside, stamping her feet and tucking her hands under her arms to avoid frostbite.

"What took you? If you were any slower, you'd have found me in cube form."

"Sorry...tough weekend," Dana said, reaching into her jacket pocket for her keys.

"Party too hard in Chicago?"

Funny how the word *Chicago* now summoned the image of Cal instead of a city. She lowered her head and briefly closed her eyes as she tried to push away the delicious memory of how it felt to have him over her...inside her. Her hand shook as she fumbled for her keys.

"Chicago was okay." Her words were both a lie and a compromise. Chicago had been magnificent and horrible, and never to be repeated. She wasn't ready to deal with someone as intense or as high profile as Cal. As she unlocked the door, she mentioned the one weekend event she could discuss with Trish. "The real trouble started with a break-in here."

"You're kidding," Trish gasped as she followed her

in. "What would anybody want to steal from the salon?"

"My sense of security, mostly." She showed Trish the stained floor and assured her that Aphrodite's Haven, Trish's newly renovated room, hadn't been touched, which was another reason Dana knew the vandalism was a very personal message. "I had to drive to Muskegon yesterday to pick up enough shampoo and color products to last me until my regular order comes in."

"Jeez! Any idea who did it?"

"The police are on it, but my money's on my ex, even if he manages to skate," Dana said as they hung up their coats.

"Mike?" Trish pondered the possibility, twirling a red corkscrew curl around one finger. "Makes sense, in a pathetic sort of way." She stopped, her eyes wide with alarm. "Not that I mean that you were pathetic for marrying him, or anything."

Dana had to smile at Trish's energetic backpedaling. "No insult taken. Besides, he was still a rat-in-training when I married him." Or maybe she hadn't been as adept at identifying the scent of a rat as she should have been.

She switched on the computer and waited for it to warm up. It had been acting a bit out of sorts lately. "Anyway," she added, "I hereby declare this a Mike-free zone. No mention of the man."

"No problemo," Trish replied.

Dana waited for the welcome screen to appear on the computer. Still nothing. She searched for visible signs of damage, but everything looked as it always had—about five years out of date.

"Come on, you beast," she urged. "Don't fail me now."

But it did. Using the Voodoo Theory of Computer Repair, she switched the unit off and gave it the evil eye.

"I'll be back in three minutes and you'd better work then," she threatened.

The computer didn't appear particularly impressed.

Dana opened the reception desk's drawer, searching for the appointment book that served as backup for the computer. She found nothing but a few bits of balled-up foil from long-eaten chocolate kisses. Groaning, she recalled that she'd taken the book with her to Muskegon yesterday to make sure she picked up the right colors and brands for this week's clients. Unless the computer awoke, she'd be running home to retrieve the book from her kitchen.

Dana could hear Trish stirring about in the back room.

"I've got Mrs. Marshall coming in at nine-thirty for a makeover," Trish called. "Rumor has it she fell asleep on the beach in Cancun wearing her sunglasses but no sunblock. Major raccoon face. Could you keep an eye on the door? I need to get my *chi* flowing before she comes."

"Sure," Dana answered, wondering what, exactly, livewire Trish did to get her *chi* flowing, then deciding she didn't want to know. She checked her watch. One minute until the moment of computer truth.

Thirty seconds early, she tried to wake up the sleeping beast...to no avail.

"This is what I get for not waiting the prescribed voodoo interval," she muttered. "Thirty rotten seconds and I end up under the desk." She stretched out flat on her back and traced the power line from the outlet to the back of the computer to see if it hadn't become loosened in the mayhem committed by her ex. It seemed tight enough. Cursing her snug red pants and the heels on the Ferragamo pumps Hallie had bought, worn once, then generously given to her, she wriggled farther under the desk to check the line between the CPU and the monitor. She was thus entangled when the bells over the front door rang.

"Is that you, Mrs. Marshall?" she called. "Trish will be with you in just a minute. Hang up your coat and feel free to change into a smock if you'd like. They're right there on the hooks by the door."

"They're not my style," replied a voice that resonated in a register far below Mrs. Marshall's soprano range.

Dana sat upright out of sheer instinct. The yelp that shot from her mouth when she bumped her head was instinctual, too. After giving her stinging scalp a quick rub, she worked her way from beneath the desk and stood.

What was it about a guy in uniform that made a woman's heart beat faster? Dana's drummed a full-tilt boogie. Of course, she possessed the mixed burden and gift of knowing the hard, muscled perfection that lay beneath this particular navy blue garb.

"Guys tend to avoid clothes with names like

'smock,'" Cal said while rubbing the garment's silky black fabric between his thumb and index finger. "It's tough to be macho when wearing one of these," he continued, giving her a slow curve of his mouth.

Since *macho* and Cal fell under the same definition in the dictionary, Dana decided his comment was an attempt to lighten the atmosphere. While it was a nice try, his effort didn't reduce the general feeling of edginess, embarrassment and hunger that seeing him created.

"We need to talk," he said, his voice now all business.

Talk. She was fairly certain she could talk. She also knew that talk was much safer for her hurting heart than any of the other activities still dancing in her mind. "I take it you had a visit with Mike?"

He nodded. "I tried to call you yesterday."

"I quit answering the phone. I've reached my bad news quota for the week."

"He has an alibi...a woman."

"No shock there. Did it occur to you that she might be lying for him?"

"It checks out." Cal frowned as though he were steeling himself to swallow some really bad medicine. "I'm going to ask you a question and you have to promise not to go for my throat."

She looked at the location mentioned. It was strong and, as she recalled, tasted slightly salty. She also remembered that he believed she was still Down 'n Dirty Dana, a reputation she'd fought long and hard to escape.

God knew that at the peak of her wildness, she'd

fooled around with plenty of guys and had experimented with things she wouldn't dream of touching now. And since she wasn't exactly guilt-free when it came to her past, she let a lot of the lingering talk in town bounce right off. With Cal, it was different. For better or worse, his opinion of her mattered. She needed him to see that she'd grown up, that she'd truly changed. The thought of further intimacy with him still scared her to death, but she needed his respect. Unable to meet his eyes, she looked at the tips of her shoes. They were almost due for a polish.

"Ah, Dana?"

"I'm listening." Just not looking...it hurt too much.

"Mike mentioned someone named Jimmy DeGuilio. He said you two were involved, and that you've had some problems."

That gained her undivided attention. "So you want to know if Jimmy is one of my legion of lovers?"

It was Cal's turn to look away briefly. "Are you having problems with him?"

She wasn't surprised that Mike had dragged Jimmy's name into this. He'd always been jealous of the relationship they'd had. "Jimmy might be my boyfriend if I were a Dan instead of a Dana." At Cal's blank look, she spelled it out. "He's gay. Jimmy's a friend from the salon where I worked, back in Chicago. He took a job in New York City to be closer to his boyfriend, so we haven't been in touch lately. And he's definitely no threat." She paused. "I have to say, if you're following up Mike's leads, I'm worried about your objectivity."

"I'm following up all leads," he replied with a quiet

conviction she wanted to accept. "The state lab has the information they need to look for fingerprint matches, but this case is low priority."

Dana gestured around her. "And this place is all I have."

"I'm sorry. I don't mean to trivialize what you're dealing with. You just need to know where you stand."

"I know where I stand. I'm being evicted, the floor of my salon looks like a murder scene, my stupid computer won't work and I'm stuck with a cop who hates me in charge of my case."

He gave her an appraising look.

"Do you have something to say?" she demanded.

He shook his head. "Nothing worth losing my life over. I'll have someone from the department contact you once we know more."

He turned to leave.

Dana felt something really close to guilt over her behavior. Granted, her life was a total mess. Her one-year plan for Sandy Bend spa domination now looked more like a ten-year plan. Plus, Mike might have had something going with that PMS comment, but she didn't need to be quite so snarky.

"Cal, I'm sorry," she heard herself blurting.

He looked back at her. His blue eyes held something that looked like a blend of regret and humor. Dana found herself riveted by the sight.

"You know I don't hate you," he said. "Much as it would make my life easier, I just can't do it."

And she couldn't bring herself to hate him. Far from it, in fact. She knew that the desire she regrettably felt was plain on her face. She couldn't hide it, any more than she could look away from the spark kindling in Cal.

The front bells chimed. If they hadn't, Dana wasn't sure how long they would have stood there, drawn by this hot, invisible pull. She looked away and busied herself smoothing the hem of her white, belly button-baring T-shirt.

"Hey, big bro," Hallie said as she strode into the salon. She unbuttoned the bright green wool cloak that was as close to a conventional coat as unconventional Hallie would wear. "Business or pleasure?"

"Business," Dana and Cal replied in unison. Dana suspected it was the only thing they'd ever agree on in their lives. She also flat-out knew they were both thinking of certain pleasures they had shared on the fifteenth floor of the Almont Hotel.

"Bummer. I had such high hopes for the two of you. You sure you won't try a date or something just to humor me?"

It was the unforgettable "or something" that still held Dana in its thrall, enough so that she was almost willing to forgive Cal for believing the worst about her.

"Shouldn't you be home watching Steve?" Cal suggested. "He's recuperating, right?"

Hallie shrugged. "What's to watch? He's had his breakfast and now he's glued to the Food Network. Funny, since I've never been able to get him to do any more than throw some burgers on the grill. He does have his compensating talents, though," she said with a very content smile.

Dana could have sworn that Cal was working up a

blush, though he was so golden-skinned that she couldn't be sure.

"Way more information than I need," he said, then escaped.

Hallie laughed as her brother departed. "He's still so easy to rattle. It just kills him to think of me married and having a love life."

"Bad topic for me, too," Dana pointed out.

"You can't say I didn't try to help."

Which was exactly why Dana would never tell Hallie a word of what happened with Cal. Her friend's intentions had been kind, if misguided.

"So, how is Steve?" she asked, seeking some way past this awkward moment.

"Fine, though cranky. The man wasn't made to be an invalid. Since we were making each other crazy, I figured I'd have a look at this floor of yours."

"How did you know about the floor?"

"Don't you mean, 'How did you know about the floor, Hallie, since I, Dana, your best friend, alternate between not returning calls and keeping my phone off the hook?'" Hands on slender hips, she frowned at the stained flooring. "A stream of people stopped by my gallery yesterday. Not to buy anything, mind you, but to see if I could add anything to the news making the rounds. How do you think it looks when I can do nothing but shrug? I'm losing my reputation for being in the know."

"Fat chance," Dana said. They didn't come any better connected than Hallie, and she used her popularity to help promote Dana's business.

"I think we can paint it."

"Paint what?"

"The floor. You really are distracted, aren't you? It's kind of a short-term fix, what with all the funky stuff you drip and spill around here, but it should do the job until you get the new flooring down as part of the big renovation."

The phone rang and Mrs. Marshall walked in the door at the same time. Dana waved to Mrs. Marshall and pointed her toward Trish's room while giving a patently false cheerful greeting to whomever was on the phone. "Good morning, Devine Secrets."

It was Mrs. Lindsay from Hart wanting to know if she could make her one o'clock a two o'clock. Her grandchildren were visiting and...

Dana dug through the desk drawer for her appointment book, remembered it wasn't there, then confirmed with Mrs. Lindsay anyway. Even if it wasn't okay, Dana had survived double-bookings before. By the time she was off the phone, Hallie was on her hands and knees scratching her fingernail against the stained vinyl flooring.

"One color or a pattern?"

"Whatever will cover the mess," Dana replied. "And nothing too hard for me to do."

"I'll give you a paint-by-numbers pattern," Hallie said. "So, in the minute and a half we have to ourselves, tell me, are you okay?"

Dana nodded.

"No, I mean really okay, not this tough chick act you use to fool everyone else."

Not everyone. Dana suspected that like his sister, Cal could also see right through her. It must be something in the Brewer genetic code that gave them this talent.

"I've been better," she said. "Know of any cheap houses for rent?"

"Cheap? In Sandy Bend? You'd have better luck asking for summer to arrive three months early."

"Well, keep an eye out because it looks like I'm being booted from my house."

"You're kidding? You're the only person I know with the guts to rent the Pierson House."

"First, it's not haunted. Well, not too haunted. Second, the owner is moving back."

"Mr. Vandervoort?"

Dana nodded.

Hallie frowned. "I'd better tell Cal. According to my dad, that man ran the biggest numbers ring on the west side of the state. He took off just before they were ready to arrest him and his girlfriend, who was the kneecap breaker of the team."

Great. Not only was she being evicted, she was being evicted by a criminal. With luck, Vandervoort's gun moll wasn't coming back with him. Dana liked her knees.

"But that was a lot of years ago," Hallie added, no doubt worried about the hysterical grin Dana could feel stretching her face. "We were just kids, and besides, you know how my dad likes to embellish stories."

Recalling her phrase of the day—*It could be worse*—Dana laughed. Maybe now it could get no worse.

6

AFTER HIS CONVERSATION with Dana, Cal retreated to the relative calm of the police station—a calm that died an ugly death when Richard MacNee strolled in. MacNee's visits had become almost a daily event. Cal knew his competition was doing it to grind down his patience and push him into a rash act, but it wasn't going to work. Too much was at stake.

Cal wasn't a twenty buck word sort of guy, which is why when the word *unctuous* came to him, it gave him a jolt. A twenty buck word—and possibly even more expensive—but damn, it fit. MacNee's smile was oilier than a Texas well.

"Seems you have yourself a crime wave going, Brewer," the man said while dusting off a coat already free of snowflakes.

"I wouldn't define one break-in as a wave, Dick."

"Richard," he corrected as his smile grew brittle and then disappeared altogether.

Cal managed to hide his smirk. Okay, so it was juvenile to call the man by a name he clearly hated. In this case, that didn't make the act any less satisfying.

"I'm sure Dana Devine wouldn't take to hearing you discount her troubles."

Hearing Dana's name roll off those greasy lips took the pleasure out of baiting MacNee. In fact, Cal found himself feeling downright territorial—not that he was too sure whether the protective impulse had more to do with guarding his hide or Dana's.

"She knows the matter is receiving my full attention."

His words were a gross understatement. Generally, he could leave his work at the station and sleep at night. Not so when Dana was involved. Both Sunday and Monday nights had been wasted attempts at rest.

What had happened to Dana was personal—not just in the vindictiveness of the act aimed at her, but in the way it had affected him. Just now, Cal couldn't afford the career risk of being seen with someone as flamboyant as Dana, but the night they had shared still linked them...maybe forever.

Cal pulled out of his thoughts to see MacNee scrutinizing him in the way only a cop—or in Dick's case, former cop—can. His smile slowly returned, then grew. It had a voyeuristic edge to it, like some lowlife's at a peep show.

"I can't imagine Miss Devine having any less than a man's full attention." Whistling an off-key, annoying-as-hell tune, MacNee turned on his heel and walked out of the station.

Furious, Cal wrestled with the idea of chasing him down and arresting him for the sheer satisfaction, but knew he couldn't get away with it. He also asked himself whether he'd given something away, whether he'd let something slip from behind the impassive expression he'd schooled himself to wear while on the job.

He hated to think that he could be read this easily by someone like MacNee, who on most days couldn't see past his own ego. Cal bracketed his face in his hands and tried to massage away the stress settling in his temples. Dana had him seriously off balance. He'd be a fool to think MacNee couldn't spot it.

Life in Sandy Bend had never been simple, but now it was downright complicated. Cal had the feeling that no matter which way he turned, he kept ending up right back on Dana Devine's doorstep.

OKAY, so life could be a little worse.

Dana watched her insurance agent wrap herself in her full-length mink coat, pull on her kidskin gloves, then turn up her collar to protect those multicarat diamond earrings before she could brave the walk to her office next door.

Missy's a client, and a well-paying one, Dana reminded herself before she gave in to the impulse to pelt the woman on the back of the head with one of the curlers she had set up for Olivia Hawkins's standing Tuesday appointment.

"Bye, Missy, and thanks for coming to confirm the bad news in person." Not only was Dana's deductible the size of a third world nation's budget, but the insurance adjuster had severely underestimated the cost to repair and restock the salon.

Missy's answering smile was a tad condescending, but then again, that was nothing new. "Anything to help a customer in need. I'll make sure that adjuster comes back here one more time, and while you're waiting, you can break open the piggy bank I'm certain you set up when you increased your policy deductible from five hundred dollars."

She paused, then sighed dramatically. "Not that you have a reputation for being prudent. I think people tend to think of you as more...*experienced*."

Whoa, a high school flashback. Missy couldn't have been more catty in her meaning if she'd grown fangs and whiskers. Dana clutched the curler she was holding even tighter. "One question, Missy."

"Yes?"

"When, exactly does one get forgiven for mistakes in Missy-land? Does the past ever die? I'd really like to know."

"I'm afraid I don't understand."

"I think you do, but just to make it clear, I'll remind you that we both left Sandy Bend High a long time ago.

"And I'd also like to point out that even if I was more 'experienced' than you back then—and I really don't want to speculate on that—not once did I steal another girl's boyfriend. Can you say the same?"

Color rose on Missy's porcelain cheeks.

"Didn't think so," Dana said. "Now, how about if we limit our conversations to current events? I think we'd both like it better. Deal?"

A reluctant, almost respectful, smile tugged at the corners of Missy's mouth. "Deal...and I'm sorry. What I said was uncalled for. I guess old habits die hard."

Dana relaxed. "It's already forgotten. Let me know when you hear from the adjuster again."

"I will."

As the bells above the door heralded her insurance agent's departure, Dana turned back to her station. Taking charge of Missy had made her downright giddy. Rebuilding her reputation with one person at a time was a grueling battle, but winnable. She smiled as she considered the possibility that Cal would be the next to see her as she really was.

Dana hefted the curler in her right hand. "And in an amazing over-the-shoulder shot from three-point range, Dana Devine shoots!" She sent the curler flying toward the door.

"And scores!"

She whirled around to see Mrs. Hawkins holding the missile in her upraised hand. There was nothing like accidentally clobbering a client to bring a woman down to earth. After an abject apology, Dana stuck to what she was good at—styling hair and pretending she wasn't daydreaming about Cal Brewer.

CAL KNEW that finding Mike Henderson was as simple as strolling into Truro's Tavern. Every Tuesday night, Mike had permanent possession of the pool table and end bar stool in the front room—the "townie" room populated by born-and-bred Sandy Benders. Cal tended to hang with the trunk-slammers in the back room, since his best friend, Steve, was one himself even though his family had been spending weekends here for generations.

Cal wasn't much for social distinctions. In fact, he thought they were stupid. He was also pragmatic enough to know that nothing in Sandy Bend changed quickly. The fact that he could straddle both social sets was probably all the evolution the town would see for the next thirty years.

Cal scanned the room. Football season was over, so the televisions strategically placed between deer heads and fishing and baseball trophies were tuned in to a re-run of last fall's NAPA 500 NASCAR race.

Mike sat at the corner of the bar. As always, he was laughing a little too loudly, almost as if he was begging for attention.

Tonight, he'd get his wish.

Cal settled on the stool next to him, but didn't acknowledge him. Experience told him to let Mike do the talking.

"Hey, Anna," he said to the bartender. "How about a Police Chief's Special?"

"Sure thing, Chief," she said, then grinned. "Thirty years behind the bar calling your dad 'Chief,' and now I get to say it to you. Sure hope it stays that way."

She wasn't alone in the sentiment.

Anna slid a tall club soda with two lime wedges across the bar. Cal handed her a couple of bucks to cover the drink and a tip. Ignoring Henderson, he drank his soda and exchanged hellos with everyone who stopped by. He could almost hear Mike's nerves humming like a strand of tightly stretched piano wire.

"You're doing this to get to me, right?" Mike finally snapped. "You figure if you sit here long enough I'm going to slip up and say something."

Cal unfurled his best "good old boy" smile. "Heck, Mike, I'm just having myself a drink and watching a little television. Don't mean to get on your nerves."

Mike took a quick swig of his beer and set it back on the bar. "That so?"

"Sure. Even I take some time off every now and then."

Cal turned his attention back to the race, though he

figured it was going to turn out pretty much the way it had in October.

"So did you check out that DeGuilio guy?" Henderson asked after a stretch of silence.

"Yeah, and it's not nice to give me extra busywork. I've got enough to do as it is."

"He could have been involved," Mike said, hunching over the bar in what Cal easily pegged as a defensive posture. "Jimmy knows all about hair salons. Anyway, lots of people have it out for Dana."

Cal echoed Mike's earlier, "That so?" He waited for a downbeat, then added, "Just to narrow the list, I don't suppose you'd like to come in to the station and get fingerprinted?"

"Yeah...sure," Mike said with no enthusiasm at all. "But you know I'm still in the salon a lot, so it wouldn't prove anything if you found my prints, right? And I had an alibi." He went to take another drink, noticed the bottle was empty and put it down.

"We could eliminate yours from the unidentified prints."

"Oh." Mike toyed with the empty bottle, looked down the counter where Anna was chatting with other patrons, and then back at Cal. "You get what I'm saying about Dana? You know her type...one slipup and you're history. I wanted to give her another chance after I broke up with Suzanne, but she said she was worried I'd die in my sleep. When I least expected it...smothered by my own pillow."

Cal fought back a smile. That sounded like Dana all right. And it was a lot funnier to hear that biting humor when it wasn't directed at him. Then there were all of the facets of Dana that Cal wanted to experience again—her sexy laugh, her sensuous touches, her lush mouth. Only four days had passed since they'd been together in Chicago. Already Cal was starving, and worse yet, knew he had to go hungry. Henderson was a fool. He'd found paradise and thrown it away.

"I don't know why I was with her in the first place," Mike grumbled.

Cal had his guesses, all of which centered on sponging off Dana's hard work, and all of which he planned to keep to himself.

"So, are you seeing anyone new?" he asked.

"Yeah, besides that Tiffany you talked to—isn't she a babe?—I've got one or two others."

"Sounds like you're over Dana."

"Like a bad case of flu," he said. Not that Cal was entirely buying in, especially when Mike added, "We'll see how long it takes her to come crawling back."

Cal made a noncommittal sound instead of the howl of laughter he wanted to let loose. Dana Devine crawl? Not in this lifetime.

SHAKING WITH TERROR, Dana belly-crawled past the living room windows and toward the front closet, where she kept all the sporting equipment she seldom used—including Mike's baseball bat. Lying to Mike and saying she had no idea what had happened to it had been sheer divorce-driven spite. That vindictive moment just might turn out to be critical in saving her life.

She'd been awakened from a nap on the living room couch by the sound of someone sneaking into her house.

The guy on the other side of the door had already managed to pick the lock and was swearing like a keel-hauled sailor because the security chain wouldn't give. Intent on protecting herself, she didn't see any point in asking exactly who the intruder was. Suffice it to say that she didn't recognize the man's voice.

Dana reached the closet, frantically dug her way to the back, and came out with Mike's cherished Louisville Slugger. Gripping the bat in both hands, she approached the door. A bony but very tan hand had reached inside. Dana dragged in a shaky breath and quelled the cowardly thought of screaming at the top of her lungs until Cal Brewer magically appeared and rescued her. Tempting, but so unlikely that she was better off coming up with a way to rescue herself.

"Try getting out of this, buddy," she muttered as she planted her shoulder on the door, pinning the evil hand.

Swearing gave way to howling.

"The police are on the way," she lied over the noise.

"They should be. You ought to be arrested," groaned the man. "You broke my hand!"

Dana glanced down. "Your fingers are moving just fine."

As he struggled and she dug in with her shoulder, it occurred to her that she was now at a bit of an impasse. If she let up on the door to go make good on her threat of calling the police, he'd be back at the safety chain, alleged broken hand and all. If she didn't let up, there was a good possibility she'd be standing here until tomorrow morning, when Trish would be locked out of the salon, and might check on her.

She needed a plan.

Dana tightened her grip on the bat. "I'm the forgiving type, so I'm going to step back. If you get off my porch and go away, we'll call it even. And if you don't, you should know that I've got a baseball bat and I'm not afraid to use it."

"A baseball bat? You think a little girl with a baseball bat scares me? I have a big, fat pack of Miami lawyers I'll sic on you as soon as I get out of here."

"Yeah, well, I know a big, mean police chief," she semibluffed. Then it struck her. Had he said *Miami?*

"Uh-oh," Dana murmured, and then leaned her head against the door. "Um, would you by any chance be Mr. Vandervoort?"

"You bet your last Havana cigar, I am. Now let go of this door so I can get my hand out."

She stepped back. Mr. Vandervoort pushed the door inward to the extent of the safety chain, and removed his hand. While he muttered about knuckle-crusher women, Dana tried to pull together her composure, but it was a losing battle.

"Are you going to open the door the rest of the way or are you just going to slip some bandages and a Manhattan straight out the crack?"

She eyed the chain.

"Come on, I drove all the way from the airport in Detroit. The last rest stop was over half an hour ago and my bladder's not what it used to be."

Dandy. A gangster who had to plan his hits around potty stops. Dana sighed. "Fine, I'll open the door, but I'm not letting go of the bat."

Vandervoort wheezed. At least, Dana thought it

might be a wheeze. She swung open the door and then held the bat at ready.

Her landlord—well, soon-to-be former landlord—was about six feet tall but weighed maybe one hundred thirty pounds. She guessed he was somewhere past seventy, but he was still pretty jazzy looking—almost like a retired pirate. His receding silver hair was pulled back in a ponytail and he had a gold hoop earring in his left ear.

"Nice pajamas," he said, cradling his scraped hand with his good one.

Dana looked down and realized that she was wearing her favorite flannel pajamas emblazoned with 1950s style buxom ski bunnies.

"Do you think you could find me some bandage and antiseptic?" he asked as he stepped across the threshold.

Fifteen minutes later, they were seated at the kitchen table. In hopes of restoring her dignity, Dana had pulled on a sweatshirt and jeans. She'd also served up a thick slice of chocolate cake with an eye to buoying Mr. Vandervoort's mood. He'd seemed pretty down when she explained she didn't have the ingredients for a Manhattan in the house.

"One question—when you got here, why didn't you use the bell?" she asked.

"I did, and I knocked and called your name, too. I saw you in there sprawled on the living room couch. You sleep like a corpse, you know that?"

Dana figured given his past, he'd have reason to know. "I haven't been getting much rest lately. I guess my body was making up for lost time."

"I would have just gone and grabbed a motel room for the night, but I was worried you were sick," he said between bites of cake. "I knocked on the door some more, and didn't even know you'd gotten up until you tried to take off my hand."

Dana winced. "Sorry, but you nearly scared me to death."

A twinkle shone in his eyes. "Then I wouldn't have to worry about evicting you."

"Nice."

He fixed her with a glare, all the more effective because of his Jack Nicholson brows. Dana saw through the act, though. "But you know," he said, "I just can't do it."

"Do what?"

He hitched a thumb toward the back door.

"Oh, throw me onto the street in the dead of winter, that what you mean?"

"Funny," he grunted.

Dana found herself relaxing. Besides the one mistake with Mike, she considered herself a pretty good judge of character. Len Vandervoort was okay. She suspected he hadn't led a squeaky-clean life, but neither had she.

"Now listen up," he growled. "Before you go thinking I'm some big softy, I have some rules. First, none of that loud rap music you kids listen to."

Dana bit back a smile. She was more of a rock and roller.

"And I like my cigars. If I want to smoke one in the middle of the kitchen while you're cooking dinner, that's the way it is."

No problem. One good "dying swan" scene complete with consumptive coughing would cure him of smoking cigars in front of her.

"And since there's the chance I'll be entertaining a lady friend every now and then, you're going to have to move to the third floor."

"The—the attic?"

"It has walls and lights and heat."

"Yeah, and stuff that no one's touched in ninety years." Plus she was pretty sure that was where the ghost of Old Lady Pierson hung out.

"If you don't want it..." A man with a clear conscience, he again dug into chocolate cake. Dana knew she had little leverage. None, actually.

"Fine, I'm Cinderella." She leaned across the table. "Now here are my rules. You make a mess in the kitchen, you clean it up. I'm paying rent—and I think about one third of what I was paying for the entire house would be fair—which means I'm not going to be your handmaiden. I get the small bathroom on the second floor to myself. Under no circumstances are you to enter it. And while you're free to entertain your lady friends, don't expect me to lie to them if you happen to be seeing more than one."

Mr. V began to wheeze, his shoulders rising and falling with the effort. At first, Dana thought he was choking. She rushed to the other side of the table while mentally reviewing what she knew of the Heimlich maneuver. He held up a hand to still her. Tears ran down his leathery face.

She finally realized he was laughing.

"More than one lady friend. Who do you take me for, Frank Sinatra?"

"Okay, so I'm a little touchy on the faithfulness thing."

He wiped his eyes and shook his head. "More than one...keep that up and I'll let you live in the attic for free."

"You're a prince among men."

He looked at her appraisingly. "I don't suppose you play poker?"

Her smile grew. "This is the beginning of an interesting friendship, isn't it?"

"Could be," said her landlord. "Could be."

7

WEDNESDAY'S GOOD AND BAD NEWS was that Dana had no clients booked until eleven. It was good because she needed the time to straighten out her living situation, and bad because she also needed cash. Desperately.

After opening the salon for Trish, she hustled back to her attic apartment to assess just what she'd gotten herself into. She instantly concluded that she was about to take on a ton more work with no additional hours in the day.

When she was a kid, Dana's favorite book had been *A Little Princess*. She'd really related to kind-hearted Sara, who had been transported from beggar girl to beloved ward. After her father died and her family had disintegrated, Dana had dreamed that she would be transported into the bosom of a family that loved her— or at least noticed her. Sadly, this miracle never occurred.

"Instead, I get the attic," she murmured, running her finger across the dusty top of an ancient steamer trunk. To the attic's credit, it was heated, had lovely multi-paned windows and was plenty tall for her to stand up in. Back in the house's heyday, this had been a servants' dormitory. That heyday had passed about ninety years ago, which coincidentally was the last time anyone had cleaned up here.

Dana supposed the room had great potential. Still, like Sara, she could use an Indian with a monkey on his shoulder to do some decorating magic. Of course, Sandy Bend didn't have anyone nearly as exotic as Ram Dass, and the closest they came to a monkey was Mrs. Hawkins's Shih Tzu. That being the case, Dana started piling junk in the middle of the floor.

"Are you up there?" Mr. V bellowed a while later.

"Yes," she yelled.

Each tread in the stairway to her new domain creaked as her landlord approached. He appeared in the doorway. "I talked to the moving company about when my stuff's going to get here, and you have a week to get yourself resituated." He looked at the pile of old magazines, books and newspapers that was now the focal point of the room. "My old buddy, Carlo the Torch, would have a field day up here."

"Carlo wouldn't happen to be coming to town, would he? I could use the help."

Mr. V shook his head. "Sorry, Carlo's booked for the next fifteen to twenty."

She laughed. "Then it's up to me."

His eyebrows arched upward like startled caterpillars. "A pretty girl like you? What's the matter with the men around here? They must be putting something in the water supply if you don't have guys lined up outside the door."

"Well, I got divorced a while ago. Since then, I haven't exactly been encouraging anyone." Except last Friday, and look what that got you, her conscience reminded her. "I'm happy being alone," she lied aloud.

Mr. V shook his head. "No way."

It was her turn to feel disbelief. "You think you know me that well already?"

"Of course I do. We're two of a kind, kid. We need to be around people. I moved back from Florida because I was tired of being alone. Truth is, there's a special lady in town I've never forgotten."

"Really?" Dana couldn't help the excited rise to her voice. She loved talking to people about this kind of stuff. That was half the reason her salon was so successful. She truly cared about her clients and she never betrayed a confidence.

"Yeah, really," Mr. V echoed. "And don't get all curious on me. I'm not telling you who it is in case she slams the door in my face. I have my pride, you know." He braced his hands on either side of the door frame and gave her a speculative look. "I'm betting you won't make it to summer without having some guy fall for you."

Dana managed to suppress a skeptical snort. "That would be one loser of a wager."

He chuckled. "Trust me, I'm pretty good at this betting thing." His expression grew more serious. "I'm willing to bet that you lead with your heart. Any guy who comes sniffing around here is going to have to prove to me he's good enough for you."

She peered at the dusty floorboards. Anything to hide the start of tears she felt shimmering in her eyes. She generally wasn't the weepy type. It had to be the cumulative effect of the break-in, the move...and Cal.

"Thanks, Mr. V," she managed to say without making a teary dope of herself.

"Think nothing of it," he said in a voice that

sounded a little thicker than usual. By the time she was collected enough to look up, her self-appointed guardian angel had disappeared.

DANA WAS STILL SMILING about the amazing contrast between her landlord's flashy exterior and marshmallow heart when just before eleven, she strolled down Main Street toward her salon. She was about a block from work when her mother stepped out of In a Knot, the town's needlework shop. Dana was trapped. She and Eleanor had made eye contact, and neither of them had looked away soon enough to pretend they hadn't.

Biting back a resigned sigh, she closed the distance to her mother. "Hey, Mom. New coat? It's pretty."

"I've had it for years."

"It's still pretty."

Her mother frowned in response.

It terrified Dana to think that someday she might look like her mother, with her brackets of perpetual dissatisfaction on either side of her mouth, and the faintly superior tilt of her nose that Dana recognized as a defense mechanism. Their bones were the same, which left it to attitude to make the difference. No problem there, since she and her rigid mother were direct opposites in the way they approached life.

She waited for her mom to contribute to the small talk, but Eleanor Devine had apparently come up dry.

"Well, I have an eleven o'clock appointment coming in, so I should get moving," Dana said to fill the gap. She hesitated, then figured what the heck, why not give it yet another shot? "You know, Mom, you can come in anytime you like for a haircut."

"Gail has been my hairdresser for the past thirty years," her mother said in a tone that made Dana feel as though she'd suggested committing treason.

Gail Webber ran a small salon outside of town, and she and Dana had a good relationship. Dana sent her the traditionalists among the local population, and Gail sent Dana the trendsetters.

"I'm not suggesting anything radical, just some pampering."

"I'd never do that to Gail."

But Eleanor thought nothing of snubbing her own daughter. A little trust, the slightest bending, that's all Dana really wanted. Just enough to know she could tell her mother she was sorry for those rotten teenage years—and beyond—without having her heart ripped from her.

Though she ached on the inside, Dana kept her smile firmly in place. "Well, the offer's open. See you around."

But she knew she'd never see her mother in Devine Secrets.

A few minutes later, boots off and work clothes on, Dana stood in the back room of the salon, assessing her shoe options. As always, her mother had barraged her defenses. She felt worn down and more than a little bummed. It was time to pull out the big guns of footwear.

"Prada," she said, and just the word made her feel better. It was so exotic and sophisticated. So *not* her mother. She pulled her beloved gray patent pumps with chunky four inch heels from their cubbyhole. She'd picked up these babies at an Internet auction site for next to nothing. Ah, how she loved technology...when it cooperated. Feeling much closer to composed, she marched to the front room, gave her dead computer a dirty look, and then prepared to give her eleven o'clock client the trendy kind of haircut a hot, Prada-wearing stylist should. If clothes could make the man, shoes could most definitely make the woman.

"I NEED A VACATION," Cal announced just after the town fathers had exited the police station.

"You just had one," Mitch pointed out unhelpfully.

"Chicago was *not* a vacation."

His brother grinned. "So it was work?"

"Keep it up and I'm putting you on roadkill patrol."

"I'd be scared...if we had one."

Cal checked his watch. "At five o'clock, I'm getting in that excuse for a pickup truck and driving to my lodge. All I need is one uninterrupted night—"

"Uh, Cal?"

"What?"

"You know that call that came in while you were talking to Mayor Talbert about the crime wave?"

Cal fought to keep his voice level as he said, "There is no crime wave."

"Perception is everything." Mitch was parroting Dick MacNee, who'd been standing elbow to elbow with the mayor. By the time Dick had finished working the man up, Talbert's face had glowed a near-lethal shade of red.

"Just go on."

"The call was from Steve. He's climbing the walls— at least, he's climbing them the best he can with a bum knee. He wants you to come out to his place for dinner and a few beers. I told him you'd be there."

"You *what?* So now you're my social director?"

"Yeah, and it's a crummy job. Other than what happened between you and Dana in Chicago, which you'll kill me if I ask about, you don't have much in the way of a social life to direct anymore." Mitch took a swallow of his coffee. "He's your best friend. It wasn't like you were going to say no."

Cal braced his hands on either side of one of the station's narrow front windows. It looked like a postcard outside, with the snow just beginning to fall. He loved this place. Really, he did. But just now, it didn't feel that way.

He turned toward his brother, who showed the minimal good sense to get his feet off the desk. "You're fired."

"From here?" Mitch asked.

Cal didn't like the halfway hopeful look in his brother's eyes. "No, as my social director. I can take care of my own life."

The jury was still out on whether he could do it without further screwing up.

JUST BEFORE SUNSET, Dana pulled up the narrow two-track road to Steve and Hallie's home, which sat above dunes spilling into Lake Michigan. Snow coated the trees arching over the lane, and the waning sun cast a fairyland glow.

Paradise, she thought. That is, until she pulled round the bend and found that the other tracks in the road weren't from Hallie's car, as she'd assumed. Instead, they were from an old Dodge pickup she knew Bud Brewer owned. But Bud was in Arizona, and she'd already seen Mitch drive by in his car as she left work, which meant...

She'd been set up.

Again.

Dana fleetingly considered taking off, but she was no quitter. The past couple of days might have pushed her to an emotional brink, but she was sure she could handle dinner without doing anything too crazy. She also refused to let Hallie think she was getting anywhere by throwing Cal into her path whenever possible.

Dana quickly checked her makeup and hair to be sure she looked okay, not that the impulse had anything to do with Cal's presence. Nope, not at all. She worked up her best I'm-so-immune-to-you attitude— that jaunty smile and confident glow in her eyes—and grabbed the wine she'd brought to share at dinner. One of these days she was going to have to remind her best friend what best friend status was all about.

As she climbed the broad wooden stairway to Sandy Bend's most impressive log home, she told herself that she could handle Cal, that she *would* handle Cal.

Hallie met her at the kitchen door, which was used in winter since the official entrance faced the lake, and the wind was howling off the water.

"Hey, glad you could make it. We've got some extra company, too." Hallie's smile was a bit tentative, as it should be, given her rat-fink status.

Dana handed the wine to her friend. "I don't suppose you're driving your dad's pickup, are you?"

"Um...no."

"Didn't think so. Cal's in there, isn't he?"

Hallie danced her way around the question. "Why don't you come on in?" The pitch of her voice matched her nervous smile. "We're just hanging out around the fireplace while the lasagna finishes cooking."

Cal was in there all right.

"You could have warned me." Dana unzipped her jacket, handed it to her friend, and then toed her way out of heavy winter boots. She longed for the security of some killer shoes to wear right now, instead of her blue ragg wool socks. And there was no point in even thinking about the red flannel shirt and jeans ripped out at the knees that she wore.

Hallie led her into the expansive family room. Dana's gaze skipped past the awesome view of the lake and settled straight on Cal. He sat on a love seat facing the fireplace. In profile, the bold sweep of his cheekbones—inherited from a Cherokee great-grandmother, she knew from Hallie—made for a sight that sent one powerful tingle through Dana.

Steve rose from his armchair with minimal fuss, given his recently repaired knee. "Glad the snow didn't stop you from getting here. Can I get you anything to drink?"

Dana froze. The last time she'd mixed Cal and liquor, it had been a volatile combination.

"Nothing right now, thanks. And if I do, I know where to find it. Why don't you just kick back and relax?"

He grinned. "Always happy to oblige."

She turned to the source of her current emotional roller-coaster ride. "Cal," she offered.

"Dana," she received in return.

Maybe one day they'd work their way up to two-word greetings.

"Why don't you have a seat?" Hallie said before flinging herself in the remaining armchair, leaving one open spot on the couch already occupied by Cal.

"Thanks." Dana served up the word with a heavy dose of sarcasm.

She wedged herself as far away from Cal as possible. He seemed unaffected by her presence, which Dana should have found a relief.

"So, why are you driving your dad's truck?" she asked him in an effort to start a normal conversation.

"Mine's in the shop." He showed her just about as much interest as she would a chess match on television.

Telling herself that Cal Brewer wasn't necessarily the be-all and end-all of men, she took possession of her full half of the love seat. Her shoulder came very, very near to brushing his. She hadn't been this close to him since...

She shivered with the vivid recollection of everything she was trying to put in her past. The heat of his muscled back under her palms as she held him closer... The hunger of his kisses...

Cal gave her a faintly inquiring look. "Feeling okay?"

"Fine."

"Good."

She had to be getting to him. How could she not,

when his mere proximity was bowling her over? Still, he didn't look especially rattled, and his calm was beginning to annoy her.

Invisibility was Dana's least favorite state. She made a show of unbuttoning the top couple buttons of her shirt to show just a whisper of the black lace camisole she wore underneath.

"That fireplace sure throws off some heat, doesn't it?" she asked him. Judging by Hallie's poorly disguised snicker, the Marilyn Monroe-esque tone of voice she'd used might have been carrying it a bit far.

Steve chose that moment to ask Cal about the town council's progress on permanently appointing him police chief.

Cal gave a mournful shake of his head. "MacNee has locked on to the mayor and the council. Until I get the mess at Dana's salon wrapped up, I'm not going to have any peace."

"Then arrest Mike," Dana suggested ever so sweetly. "You'll be police chief and he'll be where he belongs."

He fixed her with a look that should have made Dana quake in her wool socks. Of course, she also thought maybe she saw a spark of primal interest in his eyes. And then there was the way he kept his gaze away from the small amount of skin she'd exposed, as though she didn't exist from the eyes down.

"You know, I'm getting damned tired of everyone giving me their opinions. I don't tell you how to cut hair," he said in a dead-serious voice, "so don't tell me how to do my job."

Hallie sprang from her chair, grabbed Dana by the

wrist and hauled her from her spot on the love seat. "Come check the lasagna with me."

"Sure," she said, not that Hallie was giving her a choice.

"Okay," Hallie said once they were in the kitchen, "so it wasn't my best idea, inviting you both here, but could you do me a favor? Let's try to survive dinner without bloodshed."

"No sharp implements, then. And maybe you should seat us at opposite ends of the table."

"I'm not sure I should even put you in the same room," her friend muttered as she pulled the lasagna from the oven.

Dana couldn't argue the point, not when the heat rolling from the oven seemed cool in comparison to what happened to her when she got close to Cal. "I'll be good. I promise."

Hallie snorted.

Actually, dinner went pretty well until Dana mentioned her impending move to the attic.

Cal's fork clattered to his plate. "Do you know anything about this guy?"

This was the first direct thing he'd said to her since they sat down at the table. "He's fine. I have good instincts."

He glared at her.

Hallie cut in with a cheery, "Well, then," but trailed off into silence when he turned the same look of doom on her.

Cal focused on Dana again. His speech started with an alarmed "Are you crazy?" and heated up from there.

While he recounted one big rumor about Mr. Vandervoort after another, Dana reached an inescapable conclusion. She'd never fall for his face-of-stone act again. He was definitely aware of her, and not especially pleased by it.

Cal lectured, and Steve and Hallie began to nod in unison, as only married couples can. While Dana appreciated everyone's concern, she began to fantasize about covering her ears and loudly singing off-key.

"Look," she finally said, "grilled Dana isn't on tonight's menu. I'm never going to find cheaper rent than in Mr. V's attic and I'm flat-out broke. Nearly every penny I'd saved to finish the salon renovations is now going toward my insurance deductible. Besides, he's a nice old guy, colorful, maybe, but not dangerous. So unless one of you is offering free housing, cut me some slack, okay?"

She received their grudging consent, and only after she agreed to let Cal look into her landlord's background.

Hallie directed the conversation back to neutral ground for the rest of the meal. Dana kept a subtle eye on Cal. More than once she caught him watching her, too. This tightrope they walked was stretching mighty thin.

Then, while everyone was in the kitchen helping to clean up, Hallie asked, "How are you going to move your bedroom furniture up to the attic?"

"I'm not sure," Dana admitted. "I have a week to figure it out."

"Ca-a-a-l?" Hallie asked in a wheedling tone.

"No!" Dana blurted.

She could almost fend off her attraction to him in neutral territory, but in her bedroom? She stood a better chance of landing on the cover of *Cosmo*.

"Good idea," Cal said to his sister. "It'll give me a chance to check out Vandervoort."

At the sink, Dana gave Hallie a subtle elbow. A best friend refresher course was definitely overdue.

ONE WEEK LATER, Dana realized that her concern over having Cal near her bed had been vastly understated. The attic was growing smaller by the second.

"I can handle this myself," she said as she quickly smoothed her hands over the fitted sheet and got ready to unfold the flat one. "You can just go on and do whatever it was you were doing downstairs with Mr. V."

"Mr. V and I have had our chat, and I'm happy right here," Cal said.

The flat sheet refused to settle where it should. Dana bit back a frustrated hiss as she tried to untangle it. Making a bed had never been this hard. Couldn't he just leave?

"I never thought of bed-making as a spectator sport," she muttered over her shoulder.

"Maybe you should expand your horizons." He took the sheet and settled two corners on Dana's side.

"My horizons are plenty wide, thanks," she replied as she tucked the bottom in.

"Maybe. Then again, I can't be sure. I haven't spent enough time with you to make that sort of judgment."

Was he flirting with her? Did the man have no clue that she was a pro? She was the flirt, he was the stone-cold, serious cop. Except, when she was with Cal, everything got messed up.

"So what are you suggesting?" she asked as she tossed him a pillow to put in its case.

"Soft," he said. He smiled. "Lots of potential."

He was definitely flirting, and was almost as relaxed as he'd been that night at the Almont. The rest of the world began to slip away, which Dana knew was a dangerous thing.

"It's a down pillow and the pillowcase is Egyptian cotton," she retorted, as though she'd been hired to work at a department store white sale. She needed to keep grounded, remember all the reasons why falling into this moment would be dangerous.

Dana kept her eyes on her pillow. After she'd fluffed it and tucked it in place, she turned back.

He was close.

Too close.

He framed the side of her face with one broad hand. He was going to kiss her. And she wanted him to.

"Dana?" he asked, giving her a chance to protect herself from the hurt that was sure to follow, once they'd gotten past the kissing and back to the arguing.

"Yes," she whispered. His mouth neared hers. She felt as insubstantial as the feather pillow she'd just put on the bed.

Their lips met and her eyes slipped shut. Oh, how she'd missed this. The kiss started slowly, but soon became the hot and demanding meeting that still stayed with her in every waking—and sleeping—moment. His taste was as sexy and dangerous as she'd remembered, and his hands as sure and knowing as they stroked her waist and traced the outer curves of her sensitive breasts. She leaned into him, and shivered at the awareness of a need already spiraling out of control. Before she'd had a chance to savor fully the pleasure, the attic steps began to squeak.

"Hey, what are you guys doing up there?"

Cal stepped back, and Dana drew in a startled breath as she tried to find balance on her own.

"Nothing, Mr. Vandervoort," she called.

"Then I'd suggest you get your butts down here. I stuck that spaghetti in the water like you told me to, and now it's boiling all over the place."

Dana sighed. "Switch off the burner and we'll be right down."

She doubted it was going to be anywhere near as easy to turn down the heat simmering between her and Cal.

8

TWO WEEKS TO THE DAY after he'd helped Dana move to the attic, Cal sprawled on the enormous brown suede couch in front of his fireplace and watched the flames dance. He'd finally made it to his lodge, that Nirvana where all his woes were supposed to fade away. With money he'd made from some pretty shrewd stock investments, he'd built the place for just that purpose.

What had once been an abandoned barn next to a burned-down farmhouse was now fit for the cover of a magazine: windowed walls with sweeping panoramas of the field and woods beyond, heated slate floors, stone fireplace, pool table, hot tub big enough for two. And he'd been known to put it to good use, back in the good old days before anyone other than he and the woman in question cared about his sex life.

Even then, though, he'd been discreet. On those rare occasions when he had the family farmhouse to himself, he'd never taken a woman there. To Cal, the farm was tradition, practically hallowed ground. It had been in the family over one hundred years, and he hoped Brewer generations long after his would live there.

This lodge, on the other hand, was a grown man's funhouse. But Cal wasn't having fun. He stood and walked to the glass-doored beverage refrigerator under the bar counter. Frowning, he looked at the contents. Everything he liked, but nothing he wanted.

All he wanted was Dana Devine, and having her would be the most stupid thing he could do. If he was to be seen with a woman, she needed to be a conservative, mommy type—a preschool teacher, maybe—but definitely not Dana, who was a walking celebration of all things sensual.

On moving day, when he'd kissed her, he'd wanted to do much more. He'd burned to peel her clothes from her, stretch her across those sheets sleeker than sin, and lose himself in her.

He never thought he'd be thankful for Len Vandervoort's presence, but he was. Cal had been working very hard to stay angry with Dana for what had happened in Chicago. The more he saw her and witnessed the vulnerability behind her flash and sizzle, the more that carefully nurtured anger faded. If Len the Gatekeeper hadn't been on duty that night, Cal would have given in to the inevitable. And that would have been a huge mistake.

As long as Cal was unwillingly and unhappily celibate, Dick MacNee was left with only the world's smallest crime wave to raise as a banner of Cal's failings. Yep, having Len watching over Dana was good, Cal thought as he flopped back on the couch and prepared to spend another lonely night.

God bless Len Vandervoort. And God help Cal Brewer.

As April began, Dana's life took on a new rhythm. The beat was spicier than it had been in a very long time.

She was awake to the taste of her food, alive to the scent of the fresh flowers she always kept in the salon, and most of all, attuned to Cal Brewer.

For two people who should be trying to avoid each other, their paths crossed with amazing frequency. Picking up a latte from the Corner Café, walking down the street to drop in on Hallie at her gallery, she'd see Cal. It was as though they were connected on some subconscious level.

Both of them kept their greetings cordial and impersonal, but it was as though their words had taken on secret meanings.

"Having a good day?" translated to "I need to touch you again."

"Beautiful sunset we had last night" meant "Keep me warm tonight."

Early this morning, Dana had come to a decision. Her relationship with Cal had changed somehow. It would be a stretch to call them buddies, but she couldn't put her finger on a more accurate word. Given this change in their status, she felt it was okay to invite him to have sex again. Good buddy sex. Affectionate sex.

Before Cal, asking had never been an issue. Events always took a prescribed order—the guy asked, and she either agreed or didn't. None of this putting herself on the line. It was odd, though. Somehow the emotional danger added to the excitement—and the insanity. If it weren't for the fact that he could say no, she'd kind of like this.

Dana opened the reception desk drawer containing the appointment cards, and pulled one out. They were pretty cool, considering she'd designed them on her now deceased computer. Each card was the size of a small invitation and had an ivy leaf border that almost matched the paint job Hallie had done on the salon entry. At the bottom of the card, just inside the border, was the salon name and phone number.

Generally, Dana just jotted the client's appointment time and date. This time, she wrote: *Montavier Inn, Garden Cottage, Saturday 8:00 p.m.* The location she'd chosen was about forty miles north of Sandy Bend. She hoped it was far enough away that no one in town would know that she'd succumbed to Cal Brewer, though heaven knew she wasn't the first. Still, it was the kind of news she wanted to keep quiet.

She didn't have anything as fancy as an envelope sitting around, so she folded the note into a sheet of plain paper to be sure no one but Cal could read it. Before she lost her nerve, she called to Trish that she was leaving for a minute, grabbed her jacket, and then hurried down the street to the police station.

Mitch was sitting at one of the two desks.

"Hey, Dana. Nothing's wrong, is it?"

"Um, no."

His smile was the mirror image of his older brother's—killer dimples and all. "Good. You're looking sort of funny."

She laughed. "You Brewer men do know how to hand out the compliments, don't you?"

"We're regular prodigies."

She shifted uncomfortably, aware that she had to get down to business. "I have a note for Cal. Should I leave it on his desk?"

"Sure, just stick it in the In box."

Dana looked at the black tray in question. Buddy sex, she reminded herself. Just some happy, friendly buddy sex.

"You sure you're okay?"

She let go of the note as if it burned her hand. It slid across the sheer plastic and lodged in the upper right corner of the box. There, she'd done it. Dana released the breath she didn't know she'd been holding.

"Never been better," she said to Mitch. "Have a great day."

"You, too," he called as she escaped.

Dana hadn't gone more than ten yards before Mike fell in step with her. Her prospects for a great day escaping, she kicked up her pace.

"I've been calling you," he said, easily keeping up with her. "Hasn't that old fart been giving you the messages?"

"Mr. V's not an old fart, and yes, he's been giving me the messages."

"So why haven't you called me back?"

"Why would I want to? To ask you if you had a good time trashing the salon?"

He continued as though she hadn't spoken at all. "I was thinking the other day how I miss those dinners you used to make. You know, the candlelight and music—"

"You've got to be kidding. I'm supposed to call you back so you can ask me for food and sex?" She snorted. "In your dreams."

"I know you miss me...just a little."

Dana slowed. Six months ago he would have been

right. But six months ago she hadn't been nearly as together as she was today. Though she remained convinced Mike was behind the damage to the salon, she needed to end the warfare and get on with life. Maybe then he'd do the same.

She drew him by the elbow to the small, gated alcove between Truro's and a currently shuttered summertime souvenir shop.

"Thank you," she said.

His brow furrowed. "What are you thanking me for?"

"For forcing my hand so I had to leave you. And believe it or not, I mean it. If you hadn't made sure I knew you were sleeping with Suzanne, I would have convinced myself that I could have made it work between the two of us. And it never would have, you know.

"I had a few rough months after we split, but look at all I've done since then. Devine Secrets is becoming more than I ever dreamed possible, and all because you left me with a whole lot of empty time." She grinned. "So, thanks."

"How long are you going to keep punishing us because I made one stupid mistake?"

"Mike, the stupid mistake was made in Vegas. We never should have gotten married. We have this way of egging each other on until one or both of us does something dumb. It's just not healthy."

"I want you to come back to me."

She shook her head. "It's time to move on. Obviously things didn't work out quite as you planned with Suzanne, but you'll find someone."

"You need me."

"Maybe once I did, but it wasn't a good kind of need, you know what I mean? I was looking to you to fill gaps in me when I needed to do it for myself."

"You've been reading too many of those self-help books."

Dana laughed. "Okay, so I picked up one or two, but they made sense."

"I'm not giving up," he said, reminding her of a stubborn little boy who'd lost his favorite plaything. And that's what it was about with Mike—ownership. That and losing someone who'd paid his way for parties, trips and fun.

"It's time," she said, then stepped back onto the sidewalk. "Goodbye."

Dana had just hung up her coat when Mrs. Hawkins arrived for her weekly tan touch-up and hair appointment. There was something comforting about having the same client at the same time every week. It was kind of like wearing a favorite pair of old shoes with a new dress because you didn't need too much to think about all at once.

"Ready for the tanning bed?" she asked her client. Personally, Dana didn't like tanning beds, but she'd inherited hers—and Mrs. Hawkins with it—when she'd bought the salon. Sooner or later, she planned to get rid of the bed, but until then she just didn't feel right lecturing a woman with more life experience than she had.

Dana did a quick bang trim for another client while Mrs. Hawkins toasted. When she returned and was seated in Dana's chair, she made a shocking announcement.

"I want something new," Mrs. Hawkins said as she examined her reflection in the mirror. "Something hot."

Mrs. Hawkins's hairstyle was so dated it nearly had a retro quality. Unfortunately, it also rose far too high for a woman who wasn't even five feet tall.

"Hot?" Dana echoed.

"Hip, with-it, happening," her client clarified. "And no more curlers."

"Good idea." Dana had been trying to persuade Mrs. Hawkins to consider this, but the grocery store owner had a stubborn streak, so she hadn't pushed it. "Your hair is beautifully thick. Maybe we could give you a modified bob. Something soft around your face, but still a style you can blow-dry yourself."

"What about the color? Do you think I should go back to blond? Half the women my age color their hair."

"Those women aren't lucky enough to have your gorgeous shade of silver. Don't change it."

"Fine, then. Do your magic," Mrs. Hawkins ordered.

It seemed that Olivia Hawkins grew happier with every snip of the scissors. "I can't believe I waited this long," she said. "What was I thinking?"

When she finished, Dana was impressed with the transformation, too. Still, she had to admit that her client's new look had more to do with the added sparkle in her blue eyes and the pride with which she carried herself.

"Now it's time for a shopping spree," Mrs. Hawkins said while patting Dana on the cheek.

Dana helped her with her coat and saw her off. After

she was gone, Dana sat in her styling chair and spun a happy loop. Spring fever was in the air. Between Mrs. Hawkins and herself, Sandy Bend had no idea what was about to hit it.

BACK FROM HIS brief and useless vacation, Cal sifted through the contents of his In box. A stack of phone messages, the five accident reports Mitch had finally buckled down and finished, and...

He picked up piece of paper folded into an envelope. The word *Cal* was written in a clear script that could only have come from a woman's hand. He turned it over, then glanced up at his brother, "Any idea where this came from?"

Mitch looked up from the fat book he was paging through. "Yup."

Cal unfolded the paper and read the simple ivy-bordered card. A date, a place and a time. Though it wasn't signed, the "Devine Secrets" written at the bottom made the sender no mystery. He could guess her intent, too.

Could she possibly make things any harder on him? Seeing her nearly every day had already decimated his self-control, not that Dana was to blame. He'd made a point of seeking her out.

Where was Len Vandervoort, keeper of the gate, when he was really needed?

Get tough, Cal told himself. He knew what was good for his future, and what wasn't. He dragged in a deep breath and dropped the card into the wastebasket next to his desk. Somehow he managed to ignore Mitch's blunt comment of "idiot." The nuclear blast of his conscience—and cravings—was a little tougher to disregard.

Cal began to return phone calls. As he dealt with Mrs. Murcheson, who lived out on the lake and insisted that her neighbors were spying on her—snowbirds happily ensconced in Florida until late April, actually—he willed himself not to look at the ivy-bordered card or to think about its sender.

While Enid Talbert, the mayor's wife and self-appointed town queen, quizzed him on the added degree of security he thought appropriate for an upcoming high school basketball play-off game, he stopped himself from reaching down and dredging out the note. It looked pathetic among the junk mail and candy wrappers.

Turning his back on the trash can, he dialed Richard MacNee.

"So, you're finally in the office," MacNee said in the way of greeting.

Cal refused to spell out his schedule, so all he said was, "What did you call about?

"I'm asking the mayor to schedule a town meeting for next week. The people of Sandy Bend should know the crime epidemic they face. Now it's just someone like Dana Devine, but who knows where the trouble will end? The citizens need to be prepared."

Cal finally snapped. "First, I'd like you to spell out for me what you mean by that 'just someone like Dana' comment. See, I think you're implying that Ms. Devine is beneath the law."

"No parent who had a child with her in high school

has forgotten what she was like. Even today, she's a threat to moral decency," Dick blustered.

Cal snorted. "Except to say that there must be a toasty spot in hell reserved for you, I'm not going to touch that pile of dung. Let's get down to this epidemic that's got you all bothered. Over the past six months we've had three bar brawls, a dozen deer versus car accidents, a couple of domestic disputes and the incident at Devine Secrets. Even added up, that doesn't constitute an outbreak, let alone an epidemic.

"I've put up with you twisting the town council's collective tail into a knot because it suits you, but I'm not going to tolerate you whipping up fear among the people I serve. In fact, if you try it, I'm going to show you up for the idiot you are. Got it?"

Cal slammed down the phone before he knew whether Dick "got it" or not. Mitch stood and began to applaud slowly, but Cal wasn't quite done. He reached down and retrieved Dana's invitation from the trash.

"Glad to see you've come to your senses," his brother said.

Cal was pretty sure he'd just lost his mind, but the decision was made. If he had to put up with morons like MacNee, he wasn't going to deny himself the absolute pleasure of Dana Devine.

AT EXACTLY EIGHT O'CLOCK on Saturday night, a knock sounded on the front door of the Montavier Inn's Garden Cottage. Dana took one last glance in the antique full-length mirror to make sure she looked as hot as she wanted to. Red silk, black leather and stiletto heels were a good start. Frowning, she slipped loose another button at the top of her blouse. It was going to take a whole lot of attitude to hide the butterflies flitting inside her.

She opened the door and greeted Cal with a smile. "Hi," she said, stepping aside so he could enter and then closing the door behind him. "I wasn't sure I'd see you."

"For a while there, I wasn't sure I was going to come." He took off his jacket and dropped it over an arm of the old coat tree next to the door.

"I'm glad you did."

"Well, I couldn't stand the thought of you sitting here alone...waiting."

The tension gripping her heart finally released. "And now that you're here?"

He led her by the hand to the small couch facing the fireplace. "We talk."

Her laughter had more to do with nerves than humor. "I had kind of been hoping to avoid talk. We don't seem to be very good at that."

He smiled. "Point taken. So what do you suggest?"

"One night. No questions. Just us."

"As I recall, we weren't very good at that, either." He paused. "Well, at least not the morning after."

She'd expected this, and had even rehearsed some witty answers. Unfortunately, they'd flown from her head, leaving an awkward, jumbled rush of words. "I made a mistake, plain as that. I had convinced myself I could handle something I couldn't. I'm sure I have it under control now."

He sat silent, one brow arched.

"Well, pretty sure."

Still no comment from Cal. She stood, looking for someplace in the room where she didn't have a view of the bed, which was, of course, an impossibility. "Look, do you want to be here or not?"

After a moment, he stood and walked to the center of the room. Dana was certain his next steps would be to his jacket and the door. Instead, he pulled his black cotton turtleneck over his head, revealing washboard abs and all the other details that tended to make her mouth go dry. He gripped the shirt in one broad hand. "Come over here."

That, she supposed, answered that.

Going to Cal was both the easiest and the most difficult thing she'd ever done. As she neared him, he tossed the shirt to the foot of the bed. Tempted beyond reason, she laid her hand on the warm skin of his chest and felt the drumming of his heart. He settled his hand over hers, staying the downward course her fingers followed.

"No turning cold on me in the morning?"

"Only if you don't stoke the fire," she answered, nodding toward the brick hearth.

He smiled, and the sight of his dimples made her heart beat faster—if such a feat were possible.

"I've got the feeling it will be plenty hot in here." He worked his way down the row of buttons at the top of her silk blouse. When he was done, he slid it off her shoulders and rested his hands on the skin he'd exposed. The blouse slipped down her arms until it held fast at the still buttoned cuffs.

Dana shivered. Cal's smile grew as he took in the rise and fall of her breasts, cupped in a frothy red lace almost-nothing of a bra. He hooked his thumbs under the straps and slid them, too, over her shoulders. Enthralled, she watched as he leisurely explored the upper curves of her breasts, lightly tracing them with the pads of his thumbs.

She wanted to touch him, as well. Wanted it desperately. She struggled a bit against the blouse that held her arms captive. Cal chuckled at the sight. "Red silk handcuffs. On you, I like them." He ran his thumb over her nipple. It rose to his touch. "A lot."

He unhooked the bra's center closure and brushed the lacy cups aside.

"Beautiful," he said. As he looked at her, Dana took in the flush of desire beginning to climb the olive skin of his throat.

"Likewise, I'm sure," she replied.

He grinned. "You're not getting off the hook with humor. You asked me here, and here I am. Now I'm going to do everything I've been imagining over the past few weeks to that sweet body of yours."

"And I'm going to...?"

"Enjoy it, would be my suggestion." As he spoke, he held her breasts in his hands. The breath eased out of Dana's body as he settled a kiss in the valley just above the center of her collarbone.

"Well, I suppose just this once..." she managed to say in a flirty voice and was rewarded with a deep chuckle that vibrated against her sensitive skin.

He kissed her once, twice...a promise of things to come. She was helpless to stop him when he walked her backward to the edge of the high four-poster bed, then nudged her so she sat upon it, her arms still bound to her sides.

Seeming satisfied with the position he'd maneuvered her into, he smiled. "Let me get you a pillow."

Better than his word, he grabbed two pillows from the top of the bed and put them one on top of the other. He settled her so that she rested perpendicular to the headboard, her legs still dangling off the bed's edge.

"Comfortable?" he asked.

"I'll let you know if I'm not."

He smiled again. "I'm sure you will. You've never been exactly shy about sharing your opinions."

Cal slipped the red high-heeled pumps from her feet, leaving Dana in her black leather pants, and her silk handcuffs.

He ran a finger down her right instep. "No panty hose?"

"Hate 'em."

"Makes my work easier." His laugh was low and sexy. "And let me tell you, this hasn't exactly been a heartbreaker so far."

He settled one knee on the edge of the bed and moved up so he was settled between her legs, his weight braced on his strong arms. "I'm going to kiss you some more right now...everywhere I've been thinking about."

Dana's breath hitched. She could only hope he'd been thinking about some of the same places she had.

He gave her countless slow, luxurious kisses, his tongue sweeping in to ride the ridge of her teeth and then enter her mouth, foreshadowing the possession she craved. She wanted to reach for him, hold him to her when he moved away, but her arms were bound.

"Easy," he murmured before working his way down to take one nipple into his mouth and draw upon it.

The heat and wetness made her gasp and arch her back. "Yes, there," she whispered.

He lifted her breast to his mouth and opened wider, taking more in. She wrapped a leg around him, holding him in place the only way she could. Her heart pounded and her skin was damp by the time he kissed his way to her other breast and began the slow, hot torture again.

"Cal—"

He raised his head. The energy and sheer sensual intent in his blue eyes made her forget what she'd been about to say.

"Let me," he said.

She nodded, knowing that if she asked, he'd free her from her silken bonds. He kissed her neck, the line of her collarbone, the skin of her upper arms, every so often returning to her mouth, giving her a brief chance to reciprocate. Every kiss she was permitted, Dana filled with her utter yearning to touch him.

Standing he moved his hands to the button at the top of her pants. Dana's eyes slipped shut with the relief that soon he'd free her. She sighed as the zipper came down. Her pants followed the same downward course, leaving her in her red undies. And the silk handcuffs.

He touched her once, gently, on the bit of silk that nestled between her legs. To Dana, the slight pressure felt like a lightning bolt. She arched upward, asking for his caress once again. Instead, he bent down and kissed her navel, then ran his tongue to the fine lace at the top of her panties.

She almost sobbed with relief when he rose again and worked her panties down her legs to rest with her pants on the floor. He helped her to a sitting position, then reached behind her. Dana assumed he was going to free her from her tangle of clothing.

Instead, he slid her forward a bit and then resettled her on the pillows. Their eyes met.

"I said all the places..." His voice was deep and raspy with desire.

He gave her a moment to object, but she didn't. Control usually meant everything to her. It astounded her that she was willing to be held bound, to give this power to Cal.

He knelt on the floor. She tried to relax, to slow her ragged breathing, but she was too wired with need. He looked at her for what seemed to be the longest time, though Dana knew it was no more than a few brief ticks of the antique mantel clock.

In spite of the bold attitude she usually managed to carry off, she felt a hot blush stain her neck and chest. She couldn't recall another moment in her life so intimate. Instead of closing her eyes as she wanted to, she watched Cal's expression—the hunger, the primal heat.

He looked up, and their eyes locked. "You're beautiful everywhere."

This was too much. She closed her eyes and accepted his caresses, first gentle, then deeper. She relaxed and let her hips rise to meet his fingers in a natural dance she could no more stop than she could will tomorrow not to arrive. He murmured words to her. Sexy, delicious words that had her believing she was indeed as beautiful as he thought.

She drew in a starved breath as his hand ran strong and sure down her right thigh, then looped behind to grip her under her knee. At his urging, she rested her leg over his shoulder. He touched her left leg and she willingly settled it where he asked. Then he began to kiss her...*everywhere.*

DANA WAS DAMP and weak and totally boneless, and it had taken her a good long while to come down from the haze of a mind-bending climax to figure out that much. She willed her eyes to open.

Cal sat next to her.

"Hey there," she said.

"Hey."

She wriggled her shoulders. "Ready to set me free? I'll make it worth your while, big guy."

He looked almost startled, then laughed. In a matter of seconds he held her upright, unbuttoned her silk cuffs and whisked away her shirt and bra. She gathered the pillows and moved them to the headboard.

She watched as he stood and stripped out of his jeans and briefs with a blunt intent that thrilled her. He left her no doubt that they were far from finished tonight. Cal pulled a small packet from his wallet, and Dana shivered as he sheathed himself.

He came to her and settled his weight over her. "Now."

She reached between them and guided him. His head dropped as he fitted himself inside her. She could see how he battled for self-control. The thought that he'd hold on for her to be ready to find pleasure sent a rush of tenderness through her. Filled, stretched, thrilled, she drew a deep, steadying breath.

He braced more of his weight on his arms and lifted himself. "Am I hurting you?" he asked.

She smiled. "Almost...a *good* almost."

Dana watched as shock, then passion, rippled across his features.

"Unbelievable," he murmured.

She drew him down for a kiss, mating her tongue with his. This was different than that night in Chicago. It wasn't simply that the edge of unfamiliarity was gone. Dana felt as though this meant more. It was a beginning, not an end.

"Believe it," she whispered after she'd let him go.

He began to move, slowly at first, then with more force. Dana urged him on, murmuring bits of phrases that were all her mind could offer through the haze of the sheer, absolute joy of intimacy.

Cal rolled so that she was sitting atop him. Looking up at her, he gripped her hips and said, "Take us there."

His mouth curved into a hard smile of pleasure as she raised herself and eased down again. Dana repeated the motion, slowly at first, then with more intensity. Hips moving to a music she couldn't quite hear but still knew, she drew out her dance as long as she could. Hot, seeking hunger spiraled tight within her.

"Come now," he commanded.

She pulled in a breath, ready to tell him that she couldn't—not yet. But she was wrong.

All it took was a simple, intimate touch from Cal for her to shatter. Lost in her release, she collapsed onto his chest. He rolled with her again, and while she clung to him, found his own end.

As she lay beneath him, still intimately joined, he stroked her damp hair back from her forehead.

"This, we do just right," he said.

Considering all the other things they had managed to do wrong so far—talking, understanding, believing—Dana considered this a good start.

As she slipped into sleep, she gave one last, contented smile. A very good start.

9

SPRING BEGAN to make more than the occasional appearance. Trunk-slammers trickled back into town, filling the streets and shops, including Dana's. In mid-May, her two part-time stylists would return to help throughout the busy season. Until then, she would simply have to work harder—no mean feat considering that the spa renovations still consumed most of her nights.

Though they had managed no more than a handful of phone calls and passing greetings in the weeks since the night at the Montavier Inn, Dana knew that Cal was busy fielding his own problems, too. After much foot-dragging, the town council had set the first of June as the date for determining who would become police chief. These days, Cal's hours seemed to be even longer than hers. When she'd walk home under the moonlight, she'd see his Explorer still parked by the station. It was all she could do not to slip in for a visit, but she didn't dare risk it.

Richard MacNee had kicked his "holier than thou" campaign into overdrive, and Cal's competition was no fool. He'd pegged the mayor and the council as the pack of hand-wringers they were. The slightest noise of discontent from a constituent sent them into a tizzy. Right now, the discontent was at a dull roar and rising.

Through a series of strategically placed comments in the local newspaper about the troubles at Devine Secrets, MacNee had cemented his image as a man of moral resolve generally not found outside the Old Testament. He also had the fire-and-brimstone contingent in town whispering that Cal was too fond of a good time to properly enforce Sandy Bend's laws.

Dana couldn't believe that people had fallen for MacNee's act. Then again, they hadn't been at the receiving end of the looks Richard had recently started giving her. They reminded her too much of Dickie Junior's sly grin that night back in high school when he'd tried to grope her. A smile that had been forcibly removed when she'd bloodied his nose and tested his soprano singing range.

Carrying her Saturday to-go lunch from the Corner Café, Dana sighed as she walked past the police station. All in all, it was best that she and Cal avoided each other. He was safe from her reputation, and she was safe from thinking of him as anything more intimate than a guy who was phenomenally talented in the art of buddy sex.

"I'm back," she called to Trish as she entered the salon. "I got us the pasta special."

Trish popped out of her room. "Perfect. I'm starved." She pulled off the white coat she wore over her clothes while working with clients.

Dana eyed her friend. "In my next lifetime, I want Uma Thurman's eyes and your metabolism." No matter how much Trish ate—and she ate a lot—she stayed thin. Dana believed this state should violate the laws of nature. Unless she attained it herself.

"And while we're at it," she said as she zipped past the styling stations, "it would only be fair if—"

She turned back. Something looked strangely out of place. "Wait a second." She thrust the carryout bag at Trish. The two stations used only during the summer season were neat and clean as always. Hers looked wrong, though.

She drew a shaky breath. Maybe she was just imagining things. The blow-dryer and curling iron were at the ready. Sprays, gels and mousses lined the back of the counter by the mirror.

Her stomach turned to lead. "Oh, no."

Her scissors—all four pairs—were gone.

Maybe she'd put them away before she left and had just forgotten. Her hands shook as she opened drawers and riffled through the contents. Her black leather scissors case was in the top drawer, as always. Dana picked it up and unzipped it, even though by its weight, she knew it was empty. She closed it and returned it to the drawer.

"I know this is going to sound stupid," she said over the pounding of her heart, "but did you happen to put my scissors someplace while I was gone?"

Trish shifted the food sack from one hand to the other. "No, I was with my client until right before you got back. What's the matter?"

"My scissors are gone. All of them."

"They can't be!" She set the food on the neighboring station and began to dig through the drawers Dana had just searched. "They have to be here somewhere. I'm not surprised this happened. You've been really distracted lately."

"Not that distracted, and I've already looked in there."

"Well, I'm looking again."

Dana sat in the styling chair and watched Trish go through every drawer. She couldn't stop shaking. Good scissors were incredibly expensive. Perfectionist that she was, she'd never touch a client's hair with less than the best. It would cost over fifteen hundred dollars to replace her full set, and she was out of business until she did.

"I can't understand where they went," Trish said. "No one could have come in or I would have heard the bell."

Dana let her eyes slip closed, as though by not seeing the truth, she could make it go away. "You wouldn't have heard them if they came in the back door."

"Oh...right."

They never bothered to lock that door during business hours. This was Sandy Bend, after all, where everyone—and everything—was safe.

Another day, another illusion shattered, Dana thought. Fear was something she'd become accustomed to staving off, but now it overwhelmed her. She wanted nothing more than to run to Cal, throw herself into his arms and cry until she couldn't cry anymore. But that was a right reserved for lovers, not sex buddies. She needed to remember that, even if the thought hurt.

Trish's gaze met Dana's in the mirror. "What happens now?"

"I don't know," she admitted. "I just don't know anymore."

CAL FIGURED that budgets fell under the category of a necessary evil, with a strong emphasis on *evil*. The rapidly growing town needed to hire a seventh officer, and both Mitch and Eric, who'd started working at the same time, were due for a raise. Meeting these competing concerns was going to require major fiscal magic.

The phone rang. He glanced over and saw that it was the general information line. Since he was the only one in the station, he answered.

"Sandy Bend Police Department."

After a pause, the speaker said, "Cal, is that you?"

He hesitated. The woman's voice sounded like Dana's, or more accurately, as Dana might sound if her rock-and-roll personality were pared down to one note.

"Dana?"

"It's me.... Look, this isn't an emergency or anything, so I didn't bother calling 9-1-1, but I need to make a police report."

"What's happened?"

"My scissors were stolen from the salon."

"Scissors?" he echoed. She sounded way too upset for having lost some scissors.

"They—they cost a lot of money and I have to make a report before Missy can process an insurance claim."

Apparently, there were scissors...and then there were *scissors*.

"Let me get someone to cover for me, and I'll be right over."

"It doesn't have to be now."

Maybe not for the report, but he needed to see for himself that she was okay.

"Five minutes," he said. "I'll be there…promise."

"Thanks."

Cal made the walk to Devine Secrets so quickly that he barely got wet from the brief spring shower that had crept in off Lake Michigan. He found Dana standing in the middle of the salon's reception area. Her arms were wrapped around her middle as though she were trying to hold in a world of hurt. In an unnerving contrast, no hint of emotion showed on her usually expressive face.

"Are you here by yourself?" he asked.

She nodded. "I sent Trish out to Gail's Salon to pick up some loaner scissors."

He drew her into his arms. "I'm so sorry this happened, sweetheart."

"I'm okay." Instead of hugging him, too, or at least accepting his comfort, she had braced her palms against his chest.

Cal could take a hint, even if it was one he never expected to receive. He stepped back.

Eyes downcast, Dana fussed with a gold bangle bracelet on her wrist while she spoke. "I think it's better if we keep our personal life separated from what's happening here. Otherwise, everything is going to get too confusing."

What in their relationship wasn't confusing?

He still knew how to get on with business. Cal pulled out his notebook and pen.

"Want to tell me what happened?"

"I went out to pick up lunch and when I came back, my scissors were gone."

"Nothing else is missing?"

"No, not even the money I always keep in the bottom drawer of my station."

"An unlocked drawer?"

"Yes."

She might as well have tacked a Steal Me sign to the cash and left it in the open. He couldn't keep the disbelief out of his voice when he said, "Have you ever considered a cash register?"

Her eyes briefly met his. He thought perhaps he saw a flash of anger, which he'd take over this freeze-out.

"I can't afford one," she said in the same level voice.

Okay, so maybe he hadn't seen anger. "Was Trish here when the scissors were taken?"

"Yes."

"Then I'll need to talk to her."

"I'll have her stop by the station when she gets back."

"How about anyone else? Any new clients, anyone in off the street?"

"No one new."

He hesitated. "Heard from your ex lately?"

"Yes."

"When?"

"Today...earlier this morning. He stops in every few days, and when he doesn't, he calls."

"Is he harassing or threatening?" Then he could suggest that Dana get a personal protection order. Once that was in place, he'd stick closer to Henderson than his own shadow. Anything to nail the lowlife and still play by the rules.

"No, Mike's been nice lately. Kind of a creepy, smothering nice. Fat lot of good it's going to do him."

She shook her head. "Don't knock yourself out going after him. I'm sure he'll have an alibi. He's good at those when he cares to be." More than a whisper of bitterness escaped with her words.

"Dana, three people besides the woman he was with the night of the break-in corroborated his story."

"I know...I know." She let go of the bracelet, but still didn't look up. "I also know Mike's behind this."

Cal said nothing because there was nothing he could say, other than she was probably right.

"Do you have any other questions?"

He'd had more cordial conversations with felons and he wasn't sure how to fix things. "We're done for now. I'll get a copy of the report to you when it's finished, which shouldn't be more than a couple of hours." He hesitated. "I can also drop a copy with Missy, if you want me to."

She gave a small nod in response. "Thanks."

"Look," he said, "I know you're under a lot of stress right now and you don't need me adding to it, but have I done something to tick you off?"

Now he had her full attention. Her eyes were wide, and some of the wariness had faded. "You? No...of course not. I'm just trying to keep things in perspective."

Cal shook his head, wondering if he'd ever understand her. "I'm worried about that perspective of yours."

"What do—"

Her words ended on a sigh as he pulled her back into his arms and held on tight. He kissed her forehead, then said, "Just consider this a perspective readjustment from your local police chief."

"You're making this so hard, Cal," she said, but he noticed she wasn't trying to get away. In fact, she had almost melted into him.

He closed his eyes and breathed in her scent—flowers and something exotic and sexy. She had worked her way into his life. A day didn't pass without Cal finding himself thinking of her, wondering what she was doing at that moment. "I'm not trying to make it difficult, sweetheart, I'm just trying to make it better."

Just then, the front bell chimed. Dana quickly wriggled out of his embrace.

"You're in business," Trish said as she set a package on the reception desk. She gave them both a knockout of a grin. "Hey, Chief. How's it going?"

He smiled back. "Good...considering. Do you have any time to stop by the station?"

"Sure. I have a two o'clock, but I'll come over after that."

"Good."

Before Cal left, he stopped at Dana's side. One hand on her shoulder, he leaned close and promised, "We'll finish your perspective readjustment later."

Fair was fair. She'd altered his universe until everything looked different. He couldn't put his finger on the change, wasn't even sure if he liked it, but he needed to understand it. Tonight.

IT WAS PAST NINE, and Dana had just finished a working dinner of a diet cola and chocolate bar when she heard a rapping on the salon's front door.

"This had better be good," she muttered.

She was in no mood to put on a polite face and manners. In fact, she'd like to turn this place back into the Hair Dungeon, as it had been named when she'd bought it. Then she'd pull up the drawbridge and dare anyone to cross.

Dana rounded the corner to the front room and stopped in her tracks. Bathed in the glow of the lantern that hung above the door, Cal peered in the glass sidelight. He was smiling, even though she knew she didn't deserve friendliness.

She'd been with a client when he'd dropped off the report around four o'clock. Though she'd known it was the coward's way out of her emotional confusion, she hadn't made eye contact with him, or even given him much of a hello. In the face of all that warmth and sunshine, she hadn't expected him to show up again.

"I called your house, and Mr. V told me you were still at work," he said as she ushered him inside, then locked the door after him. "I had a hard time believing it, considering what you've been through today."

"It hasn't gotten any better. Missy Guyer dropped by earlier to tell me that my insurance isn't going to cover much. The theft is a new event or something like that, so I have to pay the full deductible." She shrugged. "Bottom line, I'm officially broke. There's work to be done here and from now on, no workers to do it."

He unzipped his jacket and dropped it on a chair. He'd changed out of his uniform and into jeans and a sweatshirt, which somehow made him seem more accessible. Dana relaxed a little.

"So what's on your list for tonight?" he asked.

"Well, I've got the finish work on the drywall in the Eden Room and the back hallway. Some of it is ready for sanding and the rest still needs the seam tape covered. If I can get it done tonight, I'll be able to prime the walls tomorrow."

The curve of his mouth was clearly skeptical. "It's already past nine. Anything else, like maybe build a gazebo out back or remortar all the brick on the building?"

"Okay, I know the schedule's a little aggressive, but Hallie wants to get started on the mural she has planned. Besides, the work keeps my mind off other stuff." And she definitely had plenty of that not to be thinking about.

"You know," he said, "I generally don't mention this for fear of being enlisted to help on every project in town, but I'm a pretty decent drywaller."

"You're just saying that to impress me," she said in a lukewarm effort at a joke.

"Sweetheart, I think we're beyond the point where we need construction skills to impress each other."

Had someone turned up the heat? Dana lifted the neck of her T-shirt away from her skin to get a little air circulating.

"Um...right," she managed to say, wondering why Cal—and only Cal—had this effect on her.

"So, are you going to put me to work?"

If he helped, she'd be a day closer to back on schedule. He also would have slipped out of that pen she'd mentally corralled him into earlier today, the one labeled, Sex Only. She needed to keep him where she could handle him. Well, almost handle him.

"Cal, I appreciate your offer, but—"

"Just let me do this," he said in a way that invited no argument.

Dana gave in to the inevitable. "Okay."

She led him to the Eden Room, which at present was looking more like a corner of hell. Even before this latest setback, she'd had to let the drywall installers go and do the last of the work herself.

"Got a little carried away here, huh?" Cal asked, running his hand over a seam that looked like a relief map of the Rocky Mountains.

"I did that before I figured out that less is more. At first I assumed that drywall goop was like cake frosting. You know...splat on some more to hide your mistakes."

He chuckled. "I'm not sure which is worse, calling it goop or comparing it to frosting. Why don't you grab a sanding block and start cleaning this up? I'll work on the other side of the room."

Before beginning, she went to the back room and switched on the salon's sound system. The mix of CDs, with everything from old Aretha Franklin classics to newer stuff by the Dave Matthews Band, was the beat that kept her working day and night.

Dave was singing about wanting someone to crash into him as Dana walked back to the Eden Room. She stopped in the doorway. Cal stood in profile to her, and she'd be more than pleased to crash into him. Riveted, she watched his muscles tense and flex as he deftly applied the dreaded drywall goop to a line of tape running up the middle of the wall.

When Hallie was ready to paint Adam into the garden, Dana would have to suggest Cal as inspiration. Then again, maybe not. Not only would Hallie be totally disturbed by the thought, but she had no idea that anything was happening between the two of them. The whole situation was too confusing.

He turned and faced her. If before she had felt warm, now she sizzled. Her hunger must have shown on her face because his smile faded and was replaced by an expression so intense that a shiver chased through her.

"I want you to come to my lodge with me tonight," he said. "I need us to be alone, and away from town. We'll stop at your place for some clothes. I promise I'll get you back tomorrow before you open."

Dana needed the release he offered. Actually, she craved more, but this was all she felt right in taking.

"Yes," she said.

He seemed to relax. "Let's get to work. The sooner we're done, the sooner we're out of here."

It was close to eleven when they finished. The night sky was bright with stars, and even though the sun had set long ago, the breeze held a hint of warmth. Dana had finished locking the back door when Cal swung her around and gave her a hard and hungry kiss.

"Just to tide me over," he said when he was done.

"Wow."

He smiled. "Yeah, wow."

Footsteps echoed against the building's brick exterior. Dana instinctively moved away from Cal.

Both watched as Richard MacNee approached them

from the direction of the grassy strip that ran along the river. He had been no more than fifty feet away. Dana's heart sunk. He couldn't have possibly missed their kiss.

MacNee joined them. He wore that smile Dana hated. "Evening, Cal...Dana."

"What are you doing back here?" Cal asked.

"I'm enjoying the view," MacNee said. "The river's pretty come springtime, don't you think?"

"The river's the same any night of the year—black," Cal replied in a flat voice.

MacNee laughed, and it wasn't a pleasant sound. "I'll give you your privacy. Looks like you need it."

Cal took a step forward, but Dana laid her hand on his arm. "Just leave him," she said.

Whistling a happy tune, Richard MacNee strolled up the sidewalk toward Main Street. Cal and Dana stood in tacit silence until MacNee's footsteps had faded away.

"I think it's better if I go home by myself," Dana said.

"We had a date. MacNee doesn't change that."

She shook her head and began walking. "MacNee changes everything. He'll follow us."

"So what if he does?" he asked, keeping pace with her. "He can hardly come back to town and announce that he's been spying on me. That wouldn't score him any points with the town council."

"You're not being devious enough, Cal. He'll start rumors, and come Monday morning, you'll be explaining your sex life to Mayor Talbert over coffee at the Corner Café."

Cal was silent as they passed the church, then turned down Linden toward the Pierson House. "He can do that, anyway. Besides, I think the council will still let me date."

Stubborn man. Didn't he understand that she was trying to protect him?

"If you decided to take out one of the Brogan twins or Mayor Talbert's daughter, that would be dating. If you're seen with me, it's different."

He didn't say anything in response, so Dana pressed on.

"This is all about small town vision. Everything is magnified. It's okay for people to come to me to get their hair cut or colored because they see me as wild and trendy. But would they want me at their dinner table?"

Cal swung in front of her and gripped her by the shoulders. "Stop this, now. What matters to me is that I think you're sexy, soft...special. I hope to God you can see it in yourself one day.

"For now—once I get you safely to your door—I'll leave you alone. But after that, consider yourself on notice. Things are going to change between us."

He just didn't see it the way she did. "But things in Sandy Bend never will."

AFTER SEEING DANA HOME, Cal went back to the station where he spent a couple of hours going through old files and straightening out current ones. Not exactly brain-tapping work, yet still productive enough to give him the sense that business was moving forward, even if his personal life had just slipped into a swamp.

As he worked, he thought of Dana, of her distress to-night. He'd always known that she had some issues. After all, who didn't?

He was self-aware enough to recognize that he tried too hard to be like his old man, which was why Dana gave him such a kick. She had flair and humor, but most of all, she was her own person.

But someone—or maybe more than one person—had told her she was worthless and it seemed that on some level she believed it. He couldn't do anything to fix the damage from her past, but he could stop any new poison from seeping into her life.

Cal grabbed his jacket and headed for the door. There was a seed of truth in Dana's statement about Sandy Bend's inability to change.

He found Mike Henderson in Truro's, just as he'd expected. The guy didn't look especially happy to see him, either.

"Come outside," Cal said.

He gestured at the pool table. "I'm up."

"Now."

"And if I don't feel like it?"

Cal held his anger in check. "Then I guess I'll have to make you feel like it."

Mike scowled. "Wait for me," he said to the guy at the table, whom Cal recognized as Mike's younger cousin, Andy.

"So come on," Henderson said, in what Cal considered a poor show of bravado.

"After you."

Sandy Bend could be a pretty desolate place. At one in the morning, there were maybe a dozen cars parked on Main Street, which was a good thing because Cal wasn't in the mood for an audience.

He cut to the chase. "Make Dana's scissors reappear by morning."

"I don't know what you're talking about."

"Sure you don't." The ugly glimmer of victory Mike hadn't quite been able to mask only increased Cal's confidence that he had the right guy. He was about to do something that went against everything but his heart. "Just get them back there and we'll pretend it never happened."

"Supposing, for argument's sake, I knew what the hell you were talking about and that I got these scissors back to Dana. Are you telling me that honest and up-right Cal Brewer is offering a Get Out of Jail Free card? MacNee's just going to love this."

Mike clearly didn't know who he was dealing with. "What I'm telling you is that if those scissors don't reappear, I'm through playing nice. And since you seem to need things spelled out, let me add this.... If I catch you near Dana, her salon or her house, I'm going to make you the sorriest s.o.b. to ever live in Sandy Bend. Is that plain enough for you?"

Henderson stared for a moment and then laughed. "I can't believe I didn't figure this out. You're doing her, aren't you? You and Dana have been—"

Cal's hand streaked out and grabbed Mike's sweat-shirt before the conscious thought to attack even formed. "Not another word. Not one." He wanted to send the worm face first into the pavement, but knew he couldn't, which only made the need more driving.

"We both know that your fingerprints are all over

Dana's salon. Now, that doesn't prove you're behind the scissors theft, but it doesn't exactly leave you lily-white, either. I'm going to be watching you, Henderson, because you're going to slip up and when you do, I'm going to nail your ass." He released Mike. "Now get out of here."

Mike left, leaving Cal in an empty street and with a very full conscience. He'd never lost it like that before, and he knew that he'd just done Dana far more harm than good.

Cal walked to his car and sat there for a very long time before starting it and driving home, where he should have gone in the beginning.

10

THE NIGHT AFTER the fiasco with MacNee, Dana and sleep were no better than distant acquaintances. By six-thirty the next morning, she'd already read a book, cleaned out her dresser and reorganized the collection of trunks and boxes that passed as attic decor. What made this insomnia all the more vile was that today was Sunday, when she generally allowed herself to laze in bed until, oh, seven-thirty.

Dana needed to work off her stress. It was either that or implode, and Old Lady Pierson's ghost didn't need the company. That left her with exercise. She sat on the edge of her bed and tied her running shoes good and tight. The last thing Dana needed was blisters. The only safe pleasure she had left was her shoe collection.

Testing this running concept, she jogged down the stairs. Before stepping out the door, she tugged the zipper on the top of her gray sweats a bit higher to protect her from the morning chill.

After a few perfunctory stretches by the front steps, she was on her way. She made it as far as Main Street before the stitch in her side began to feel more like an ax. Maybe if she ran more than once a year...

When she'd caught her breath, she picked up her pace from a dead halt to a leisurely stroll and headed toward one of her favorite thinking spots—the marina.

The place reminded her of her dad. When she was little, she'd sneak down on summer days and follow him around as he worked.

This early in the season, Journey's End Marina was a quiet spot—especially before seven in the morning. The only sounds were the seagulls' cries and the chiming of the sailboats' rigging as the breeze wove through them. No people, though. Most trunk-slammers seemed to believe that the good weather started only after Memorial Day. The charter fishermen knew better, and had already left with their passengers to haul in a good catch.

Dana wandered through the yard, which was a maze of boats not yet in the water. She reached the picnic area by the docks and sat on one of the tables, her feet on the bench. She smiled at memories of her father sitting here swapping fish stories with the guys. What would her dad think of Cal Brewer? she wondered. Dana suspected he'd like the man Cal had become. She sighed, contemplating all the ifs in life.

If her father had lived...

If she hadn't fallen for Mike...

If MacNee hadn't seen her kissing Cal last night...

She couldn't fix any of them. All she could do was keep moving forward with the same determination she'd shown over the past year. Dana stood. She was about to leave when, between two rows of cradled boats, she saw Cal heading her way. He had one hand tucked into the pocket of his tan jacket. In the other he carried a bag.

"Hi," she said as he neared. "What are you doing out this early?"

"Probably about the same as you." He settled the brown grocery sack on the picnic table. "I couldn't sleep."

Dana entertained a brief vision of the two of them curled up in bed, finding comfort in the other's closeness. Without thought, she placed her hand on his chest, seeking the steady beat of his heart. He folded his fingers over hers, lifted her hand to his mouth and kissed it, his lips warm against her chilly skin.

"Are you okay?" he asked.

She nodded. This stolen moment certainly helped. "After I gave up on sleep, I thought maybe I'd try some exercise."

He smiled. "When you were on Main Street, I didn't see you moving any faster than a stroll."

"I guess when it comes to stress release, meditation's more my style." She drew in a breath of crisp, morning air, then slowly released it. "You know, getting your mind in a good place, and all that."

"I'll stick with an hour in front of a punching bag."

She had to admit that sounded like a plan, too.

"Maybe I can help with the stress," Cal offered. He gestured toward the package he'd left on the picnic table. "Look in there."

Dana unrolled the sack's top where it had been folded over several times, then peeked inside. Silvery objects shone at the bottom.

"My scissors!"

She pulled out her favorite pair of six-inch, offset shears and turned them over in her hands. They'd probably need a little TLC after knocking against the other blades, and—

Suddenly, the obvious question struck. "Where did they turn up?"

He looked over her shoulder and out at the harbor before answering. "At the police station," he replied almost unwillingly. "I found them on the sidewalk by the front door."

A gull laughed its raucous cry. As Dana tucked the shears back into the bag, she commented, "So they magically reappeared?"

Again he hesitated. "Pretty much."

He was dwindling to two-word answers. She'd probably never know how he had accomplished the feat of the reappearing scissors, and wasn't so sure she really wanted to, anyway. It was enough to feel grateful and relieved. She ran her fingertips over the smooth, recently shaved skin of his cheek.

"Thank you," she murmured.

He smiled. Dana was about to kiss him as she yearned to, when another set of footsteps echoed across the yard. She let her hand drop and stepped back. Ed Malone, who had taken over the marina after Dana's dad passed away, appeared from between two sailboats.

"Morning, Chief," he said to Cal, who returned his greeting. Ed's smile widened as he took in Dana. "I should have known it was you down here. Did you come back for a visit?"

Years ago, after she'd committed some act she particularly regretted, she would come here to clear her head. Ed always gave her the space to heal herself. "I hope you don't mind."

He shook his head. "You know you're welcome here

anytime." He looked at Cal, then back at her. Realization dawned on his weathered features. "I think I'll just head on over to the Corner Café and see if they're open yet. You two can, ah, carry on."

Ed left, and Dana sighed as the magic of the morning began to slip away. She knew she was safe in having Ed Malone aware that something simmered between Cal and herself. But thanks to Richard MacNee, the chance remained that the whole town would soon share in the news.

Biting back another sigh, Dana picked up her bag of scissors and began to leave the marina. Cal fell in step beside her.

"What are you doing?" she asked.

"Walking you home."

"Didn't we have a discussion about this just last night?"

"You made a speech. I unwillingly listened."

She scowled. "You really need to steer clear of me."

"No can do."

She figured it would take a graduate degree in psychology to learn what made Cal Brewer tick. Since all she had was beauty school and a community college course in accounting, she didn't bother. Salvaging the situation the best she could, she made sure there was a wide swath of daylight between Cal and herself as they walked.

"It looked like old Ed Malone has a soft spot for you. I've never seen him smile that much in all the years I've known him," he said after a minute.

"He was the only business owner in town who

would let me out of his sight while I was on his property."

"Maybe the Goth makeup scared everyone else," Cal suggested.

She shrugged. "Probably. Not that it matters now."

But they both knew that on some level it did, and more than it had when she'd been fourteen. Dana rounded the corner onto Linden and smiled at the sight of Pierson House.

"It's beautiful, isn't it?"

"Sure, if you want to spend your life scraping and painting all that trim."

She laughed. "So much for your reputation as a romantic."

Once they were on the front porch, she fumbled for the doorknob with her free hand.

Cal closed his hand over hers. "Give me a second."

Dana looked up and down the street. If anyone was watching, it was from behind their curtains.

He cupped the side of her face with his hand. It felt warm against her cold skin, which, she told herself, was the only reason for the tingle chasing down her spine and turning her knees to mush.

"I need to do this."

His mouth brushed against hers so briefly that the primary emotion to register was disappointment. He drew back far enough to look into her eyes.

"Not enough for you, either?"

He didn't give her time to answer. This time, it was the sort of kiss Dana craved. The sort of kiss that kept her awake well past the time her body demanded sleep. The sort of kiss she didn't dare risk.

"You taste so good. I miss you," Cal murmured before tasting again.

Her knees were giving way entirely. He walked her backward until she was leaning against the big oak door. She could feel him tugging the zipper of her sweat top downward. His pleased sound of surprise when he discovered that the sports bra was all she had on beneath it vibrated through her. One broad hand cupped her breast. She could feel her nipples harden beneath the stretchy white fabric. His thumb brushed against her and she shivered with pleasure. She didn't want to break the spell, to remind him—and herself—that they couldn't afford this.

Cal leaned his forehead against hers and slipped his hand inside her sweatshirt. "Come with me to the lodge this afternoon."

Be strong, she told herself. *Do the right thing.* "I—I promised to meet Hallie."

"Cancel."

His fingertips played ever so lightly over her left breast.

She swallowed hard. "And I need to prime the Eden Room's walls."

"I'll do it tonight. Just come to the lodge with me for the day."

He pulled her closer, nudging his knee between her legs.

"You're playing dirty, Brewer."

"I'm playing to win."

And he succeeded.

AS THEY DROVE toward his lodge, Cal smiled at the way Dana kept looking over her shoulder.

"Sweetheart, this road runs dead level and straight for miles. If anyone were behind us, I'd know."

"Okay, I'll stop," she said, but never quite pulled it off. In fact, Cal wasn't sure she even noticed what was in front of her until he was leading her through the lodge's door.

He almost felt nervous, which was something that hadn't happened around a female since he was thirteen. The degree to which he wanted her to like this place was embarrassing.

Cal gave her a quick tour of everything but his bedroom, avoiding that because he knew he'd be too tempted to stay. And while he had every intention of making love to her today, a little togetherness was going to come first. Her comment this morning that he wasn't a romantic had started him thinking. Maybe he wasn't, but he'd like to be...with her.

"I can't believe this was once a barn," she said when they were back in the living room. "I mean, I see the rafters overhead, and they've obviously been here forever, but everything else... It's even more incredible than I've been told."

His pleasure in her reaction was replaced by a vague sort of alarm. "Told by whom?"

She laughed. "You think guys are the only ones who talk about their sex lives?"

He'd been pretty happy nurturing that delusion.

"I run a salon. All day long women talk to me. It's cheaper than therapy."

"So what do they say about me?" As soon as he asked, he wasn't really sure he wanted to know.

She didn't look at him as she spoke. Instead, she ran

her hand across the back of the couch and then walked toward the bank of windows looking across the fields. "That you're a considerate lover, and that you're so smooth in the way you break up with them that they don't even realize it's happened until a few days later." She paused. "I really don't want to talk about this."

She looked so beautiful to him, with the sun shining in, lighting the gold of her hair. And so vulnerable, too. He didn't have the words for what he wanted to say. In fact, he didn't have a grip on the feelings that were driving the need to say something. "It's different with us."

She turned away from the window. Her smile was bright, but it didn't reach her eyes. "I know."

This wasn't going the way he wanted. Instead of the walls between them coming down, Dana was refortifying. "Let me make us some lunch," he said.

"You cook?"

She looked so shocked that he laughed. "If I don't want to starve, I do. Mitch, my dad and I have a pact. We all fend for ourselves. Come into the kitchen, and I'll show off for you."

He made them a pretty simple meal—scrambled eggs with slivers of smoked salmon, a salad and some white wine. As they ate at the table for two tucked in the corner of the kitchen, he tried for some way to learn more about her past, to come to understand her but still not get accused of giving her the third degree.

Finally, he told her what it was like growing up in a house full of guys with poor Hallie the baby of the family. When he asked about her brother and sister and how they'd gotten along growing up, she asked him how he'd managed to get heat beneath the stone floor.

When he tried to redirect the conversation by talking about her dad, and what a great guy he'd been, she stood and started clearing the table, then asked where he'd found the two-drawer dishwasher.

He was beginning to sense a pattern.

Cal lapsed into silence as he finished scrubbing the skillet. He could feel Dana watching him. Waiting.

"Want me to build a fire?" he asked when the last of the dishes had been put away. Relaxing in front of a fire was romantic, maybe conducive to a little talk.

"No."

"A walk through the fields, then?" Women seemed to like walks.

"Don't think so..."

She came to him and unbuttoned his shirt, pulling it loose from his jeans. She was good with her hands, and her mouth, too, he thought as she ran a line of hot, wet kisses down his stomach.

Her hands closed over his belt buckle. Cal closed his eyes and tried to regain some semblance of control.

"I want to see your bedroom," she said. "Now."

Talk could wait.

WHEN CAL SETTLED her in the middle of his enormous bed with its hewn-log headboard, Dana acted on sheer need and instinct. If, as she intended, this was to be one of their last times together, she wanted it seared into her memory. And his.

She knelt on the mattress's cushioned surface and made her way to the edge. Cal still stood next to the bed. His chest rose and fell in a hard rhythm. She hooked her fingertips into the waist of his pants.

"Let's get you out of these clothes," she murmured as she smoothed the shirt from his shoulders. He helped send it to the floor. She worked his belt buckle, and then slowly opened the copper rivet that waited on the denim beneath. Even more slowly, she eased down the zipper.

"You're killing me," he said.

"Am I?" She smiled as she pushed his jeans down his hard flanks. "I'm just getting warmed up."

He toed out of his shoes, then shucked his jeans the rest of the way off. When he stood, she worked one fingertip beneath the white elastic of his briefs. She shivered at the tactile pleasure of touching the smooth head of his arousal. She withdrew her hand and touched her finger to her tongue. His male scent and taste aroused her, and she fought hard to maintain her edge of control.

"I think I'm still hungry," she whispered.

He groaned.

She urged him onto the bed, then knelt over him. "Where to start? Here, maybe?" she asked, and then kissed his neck, flicking her tongue against the salty skin.

"Or here?" She suckled his bottom lip, then adjusted her mouth to kiss him fully, deeply.

"Or how about..." She caressed a path down his muscled torso, smiling at the rapid-fire beat of his heart.

Her own heart dancing faster, she kissed her way to his thighs. "I don't know...It's still not enough."

He lifted his lean hips as she slid his underwear off. Their eyes met—his glowing with banked passion—as she dropped his last garment from the bed. She stood and removed her own clothes. She could feel the heat of his gaze touching each new bit of exposed skin.

She returned the favor, letting her line of vision follow the course she meant her lips to take. He was gorgeous...fit, strong, made to love and create new life.

"You're a regular banquet, Cal Brewer." Dana ran her fingertip across his chest, past his navel and into the dark hair at his groin.

"The possibilities are um, boundless," she teased as she circled her palm around his erection.

"Dana..." The word was part warning and part plea.

She bent and kissed him. Cal's hips arched off the bed, and he groaned. Ah, but she was truly just beginning. His hand cupped the back of her head as she deepened her mouth's embrace. She loved giving him this pleasure, loved feeling the answering tension deep in her own body.

He murmured sexy words to her, hot words, begging words. She took them all in, as she'd taken in him. This, she was sure never to forget, no matter how many years she lived without him.

Just when she was certain she was about to find her release by tasting him, loving him, his fingers tensed against her and he rasped, "Stop!"

Almost dizzy with passion, Dana rolled to her side. He drew her upward and kissed her deep and hard.

"You're the most amazing thing that ever happened to me," he said. Her throat tightened with emotion. She wanted to tell him the same thing, but couldn't. Not when she planned to save him from MacNee by walking away tonight. As she struggled to regain her composure, Cal leaned over her, opened the nightstand drawer and took out a box of condoms.

"Let me," she said as he pulled a packet from the box. She brushed her fingers against his erection. It was hot and damp from her attention.

He drew in a hissing breath. "Don't, or we'll both regret it." He quickly rolled the condom into place.

Before Dana could even figure out how she'd gotten there, she was flat on her back and he was thick and hard inside her. He flexed and withdrew, then pushed his way back in. She gasped. His expression was almost a smile, but somehow an expression of hunger, too.

He cupped her bottom, positioning her hips until they met him perfectly. They found a rhythm. Again and again he came into her, until she was so close to falling over the edge that all she could do was cry his name. She turned her face into the pillow, trying to gather the strength to handle the storm to come.

"No. Look at me. I want to see you come."

Dana gave herself up to him, and they arched and peaked together.

Later, as they lay there, their limbs tangled and souls meshing so perfectly, she admitted the truth to herself. She was strong, but not strong enough to give up Cal Brewer.

11

DANA COUNTED April's passing days by her growing to-do list. Far before she was prepared, May arrived. On the weekends, the town was packed with tourists, but her day spa remained unfinished. Watching all that money march right past her doorstep was killing her. Cal kept offering to help, and she kept refusing. One of them had to keep a grip on the big picture. It looked as though it was up to her.

Before opening for business, she needed to get the two private shower rooms finished off. Luckily, all the major work—electrical, plumbing and the tiling of the steam showers and tubs—had been completed before her plan had been blown to smithereens. If she could just hire someone to lay the floor tile, she knew she could recoup the money in a matter of days.

Her banker hadn't been very impressed with her logic. He had been more concerned about her ability to repay her outstanding loan, considering the number of times Devine Secrets had recently shown up in the newspaper's Police Beat column. Telling him that Mike's idiot cousins had buckled under increasing police pressure and last week confessed to the initial vandalism incident didn't help, especially since Mike still walked the streets a free man. One dim hope remained.

Dana had known about the money from Grandmother Devine for years. When her sister, Catherine, was accepted to medical school, their mother had looked skyward and given thanks to Grandmother Devine. When her brother, Josh, had decided to study abroad after college, Grandmother Devine was again blessed. But when Dana had asked for help paying for beauty school, she was told that times were tough.

Rather than push it, she had taken a night job as a cocktail waitress on Rush Street. Tips were good and she'd become talented at fending off the gropers. She'd quit once she'd gotten her first salon job. As adept as she was at avoiding wandering hands, she decided she'd rather eat less than put up with them.

Dana felt incredibly proud of what she'd accomplished on her own. She had never again asked her mother for money. Now she had no choice. Today, she was conducting a stealth mission. If she gave her mother advance warning of what she wanted, she'd be greeted by a tidy note filled with excuses taped to her mother's front door.

After taking a moment to push back the galling feeling of failure over having to go begging, Dana rang Eleanor Devine's doorbell. Theirs was not a "drop by anytime" relationship.

Her mother pulled aside the white voile curtain covering the door's half window. Displeasure quickly replaced the curiosity in her expression. The door opened slowly, grudgingly, and just enough for Eleanor to peer through.

"Hey, Mom. Hope you don't mind that I dropped by."

"Hello, Dana."

The door opened no wider.

"I have something I need to talk to you about. Maybe you could let me in."

Sparrows chattered, a car drove down the street, but her mother was silent.

"Five minutes," Dana bargained, hating that she had to do this.

"Fine, but no longer. I'm due at the country club to help with the Spring Benefit committee."

"No problem."

Her mother opened the door. Dana stepped in and waited to be ushered to the kitchen or somewhere. Instead, they stood in the entryway, with all the cross-stitched fluffy bunny artwork her mother loved.

"Well?" Eleanor asked.

"Can't we sit down?"

Her mother huffed an impatient breath and checked her watch. "If you insist."

After they were seated at the kitchen table, Dana cut to the chase. "I've thought of every way around this that I could, but I've come up blank... I know you've heard about the troubles I've had at the salon, and I've reached the point where I need a little help to get the renovations done on time." She dragged in a breath and then said, "Mom, could I use some of the money Grandmother Devine left us?"

"What money would that be?" her mother asked through razor-thin lips.

"You know...the money you used to help with Catherine's and Josh's school expenses." She pushed on in the face of her mother's stony silence. "I remember

Dad telling me I never needed to worry about college because Grandma had taken care of that. I know things were tight when I left for school, but maybe now—"

"Do you have any idea what medical school costs?"

"No."

"Or a year of studies at Oxford?" Her mother shook her head. "Of course you don't because you didn't have the brains or the ambition to get ahead like your sister and brother. Your grandmother's money is long gone, and even if I had a million dollars sitting in an account, I wouldn't risk a penny of it on you."

"But she left it to me, too. Dad said so."

Lines of bitterness marked Eleanor's face. "Your father said many things. After the grief and embarrassment I've suffered because of your behavior, you're entitled to nothing."

"Why are you doing this?" The question was more a kind of emotional reflex than really wanting to know, because Dana had heard this speech before.

"Where do you want me to start? In high school when I had to deal with the other mothers' whispers about your promiscuous behavior, and with you sneaking in at all hours, or worse yet, not coming home at all?

"Then again, maybe you'd like to discuss current events, since you've decided to ruin Cal Brewer's life just as you ruined Mike's. And don't give me that shocked look. I heard about the two of you making a spectacle of yourselves down by the river."

Dana wasn't feigning shock. If her mother had heard about Cal, the story had traveled far. Eleanor clung to the fringes of the Westshore Country Club clique, locals who outsnobbed the snobbiest. Generally, they cared only about trunk-slammer affairs. Townies fell beneath their notice, though, ironically, the clique itself was included in that group.

"Cal's a friend," she said.

"If you were really his friend, you'd leave him alone. He has a chance to be something."

As much as Dana had changed, her mother would never see it.

"Let's just stop here," Dana said. "Forget I asked you for help. I must have been out of my mind." As she left the kitchen, she said, "I'll see myself out."

DANA DROVE to Cal's lodge just past ten that evening. The night was wet and heavy with a rain that had begun to fall in early afternoon, and hadn't stopped until recently. Thankful she wasn't being followed, she wound down the dark country road. Because it was late and the deer were active, she kept a careful eye for them. Out here, the locals said it was always the one you didn't see that blindsided you.

The same could be said for her conversation with her mother. She thought she'd been prepared for rejection, but she'd been wrong. Letting go of one's last hope was never easy, or painless.

Even hours of work in the salon had done little to take the sharp edge off her ache. She'd always known that her mother had little use for her. She had sensed it from the time she was a child. While it had hurt and confused her, she'd had refuge with her father. He had loved her unconditionally, encouraging her to choose her own star and reach for it.

After he'd died, she'd been adrift. Her mother had been too caught up in her own anger that he'd had the nerve to die to pay attention to Dana. Dana had done her best—and worst—to get just a moment's notice. Her worst always seemed to do the trick. In a way she could understand why her mother was now incapable of seeing that she'd made something of herself. What hurt was the knowledge that Eleanor Devine wanted her to fail.

Dana pulled up in Cal's drive. Just seeing his lights on made her feel better...warmer, somehow.

By the time she'd parked and made it to the door, he was waiting for her. When he hugged her, she couldn't quite make herself let go. It wasn't fair or safe to seek comfort from him, at least the kind she wanted, but she couldn't help herself.

He tipped up her chin and looked into her eyes. "You okay?"

She nodded and stepped out of his embrace. "Let me get my shoes off. I'm getting mud all over your floor."

"I'm not worried about my floor," he said as he took her jacket from her and went to hang it up. "Now, you, on the other hand, I'm worried about."

Once her shoes were off, he pressed a mug into her hands. "Hot chocolate, with a little extra kick," he said at her questioning look. "Now come sit by the fire."

Dana could think of no place she more wanted to be. She settled next to Cal and sipped her drink. The slight taste of peppermint picked up the soothing smoothness of the chocolate. "It's wonderful," she said.

"Thanks. Rough day at the office?" he asked, just as one spouse would ask another—one of those nuances of emotional intimacy she knew so little about, and was so scared to learn. Dana felt tears well in her eyes.

"The usual," she said, trying to match his light tone.

"Somehow, I don't think so."

She was afraid to say anything, because if she did, the floodgates would burst and everything would rush out—the knowledge she wasn't worthy of her mother's love, the fear that she was falling in love with Cal and the terror that everything she'd fought so hard to make her own was slipping away.

"It's nothing. I'm...I'm..."

The tears started, and once they did, there was no stopping.

Cal took her drink from her and set it on the coffee table. He wrapped his arms around her. How she had needed this, possibly even more than she'd realized.

"It's going to be okay...whatever it is," he said.

Wrapped in his arms, it was easy to believe that might be true. As the tears stopped, Dana began to talk....

CAL WATCHED as Dana slept on the couch, curled up against him. He had wanted to know her past, what drove her, and now he did. The knowledge was almost a physical ache.

He had always taken the love of his family as a given. Mitch and he might not always see eye to eye, and Hallie worried that he was turning into some sort of emotional fossil, but no matter what, they were family. For all that Dana had two siblings and a mother, she was as alone as a person could be. Until now.

She had him, whether she was willing to accept it or not.

Other than the close encounter of the MacNee kind, no one outside of his family had seen him with Dana. Cal figured there were two ways to conduct a life: in the shadows, like Richard MacNee and his worming around, or out in the open. Stepping into the daylight could well lose Cal the job as police chief, but it would salvage his self-respect. With luck, it would also gain him the love of Dana Devine. And that was worth any price.

DANA JOLTED out of an exhausted sleep. Around midnight, Cal had made sure she got home safely. Now it was... Actually, she had no idea. She squinted at the numbers on her alarm clock. Okay, not quite past one.

Something had awakened her. The trick was to sort out whether the sound had been part of a dream or part of reality. She lay as still as possible, listening for any unusual sound. After a few strained moments, she convinced herself it was nothing, and settled back against her pillows. As her eyes slipped shut, it rang out again...a woman's distant, ghostly laughter. Dana shivered. She'd thought she heard random footsteps every now and then, but never this. The sound died away.

"There's no such thing as ghosts," she whispered as much for her own benefit as that of the spirit that was having such a good time giving her the creeps.

The sound drifted upward again. Dana frowned. When she thought she'd heard footsteps, they had seemed to come from the attic, and all had been quiet since she moved up here. She folded back the covers, stood and tiptoed to the stairs. The door at the bottom was open a crack, and light shone through it.

"Weird," she murmured. Mr. V was always asleep by now. Curious, she walked down and pushed open the door the rest of the way. The woman's laughter—clearly of this world—sounded again.

She knew that voice.

Dana tiptoed to the landing halfway down the main stairway. There, in the living room, she saw something more out of this world than the ghost of Old Lady Pierson. Olivia Hawkins and Mr. V were slow-dancing in the middle of the room. The fact that they had no music didn't seem to bother them at all. Mr. V was looking at Olivia as though she were the most marvelous, incredible surprise.

Dana hungered for that kind of love.

She wanted to be able to look at Cal that way, to let everything blossoming in her heart show in her eyes. But that heart also ached with the knowledge that her mother was right.

She was a bad risk in love, and the last woman someone in the public eye needed. Dana felt her eyes tearing up as she thought about what she was missing.

To be like the lovers dancing downstairs would be paradise.

She stood there in her ratty sleep-shirt, weepy eyes and messy hair, gripping the railing and wishing with all of her heart. After a moment, and without once looking her way, Olivia said, "Everything's all right. You can go back to bed now, dear."

Dana managed an embarrassed "okay," before high-tailing it to her attic.

Olivia Hawkins and Mr. V. Dana Devine and Cal Brewer. Dana wasn't sure which couple was more unlikely.

CAL HAD TAKEN a page from Dana's book: He had a plan. And it wasn't a bad one, if he said so himself. A week had passed since the night she'd finally opened up to him. In that week he'd had flowers delivered to the salon and to the Pierson House daily. He'd helped her with the last details on the day spa rooms, refusing to be chased out just because she was worried someone might see him. And when they were alone, he'd talked with her for hours on end. It seemed as though now that she'd started, she had a lifetime of stuff to get out. He never thought he'd feel so damned lucky to hear a woman talk.

Tonight, he'd begin the final phase of his plan, which involved champagne, formal clothes and slow dancing. For any woman but Dana, attending the Westshore Spring Benefit would be a no-brainer.

But Dana was...well, *Dana*. Proud. Determined. Stubborn. Make that very stubborn.

The Spring Benefit was an annual party held at the Westshore Country Club, an exclusive old property just outside of town. In theory, it was a fund-raiser for local charities. In practice, it was the warm-up event for Sandy Bend's summer social season. Everyone converged for one huge blowout.

Cal wasn't a "club" kind of guy, but he had attended the party every year since he'd graduated from college.

Usually, it was no big deal. He'd simply ask the woman he was dating, rent a tux and be done with it. This was no normal year, though. He had to somehow convince Dana to be seen with him not only in public, but at one of the biggest events of the season. A pretty tall order since he couldn't get her to sit at a table for two at the Corner Café.

Tonight, he'd brought a bottle of wine, some brie and a loaf of French bread for dinner. He and Dana set up a makeshift dining area in the Eden Room, whose walls were now a lush, exotic jungle, with vines growing up to the ceiling. His baby sister knew her stuff, all right.

"Thanks for bringing food," Dana said. "I think I forgot to eat lunch."

He smiled at the idea. It had to be a female thing. Guys never forgot to eat. "So you're not sure if you ate?"

"It was a busy day. How about yours?"

"Nothing out of the ordinary." He paused to have a swallow of his wine. "That is, if you don't count helping to round up two of Abe Calhoun's llamas. They were heading south on US-31 with an eye to get back to Peru."

She laughed, as he'd hoped she would. "You got 'em?"

"Yep, they're captive once again." About a dozen corny lines came to him about how she held him captive. True enough, but even he couldn't push this new, romantic Cal that far.

"Hey," he said, giving her a crooked smile, "I've been thinking..."

Her blond eyebrows arched as she waited for him to go on. "And?"

He'd never thought it would be this rough to ask a girl to a dance. "The Westshore Spring Benefit is coming up, and I was wondering if you'd like to go."

Maybe he should have waited until she wasn't sipping her wine. "You mean the charity party at the country club?" she asked once she'd finished coughing. "You're kidding, right?"

"Actually, no. I thought it might be fun to get dressed up, drink champagne and dance. We haven't danced together since Chicago, you know."

He saw a quickly extinguished flash of yearning in her eyes.

"That event is organized by a bunch of social dinosaurs," she said.

She wanted to go, he was sure of it. Otherwise, her voice wouldn't waver that way, and she'd be able to meet his eyes. "They're nice dinosaurs. Really."

"It's just not my thing. Why don't you go without me?"

"Because I want to go with you."

She moved aside her wineglass and stood. She looked almost scared.

"It's taken me a lot of years to build up an image as Sandy Bend's bad girl. You want me to give back all those gains by showing up at a public function with you?" She laughed. "I don't think so, Chief."

He felt a jolt of shock as strong as if she'd hit him. It took the full sum of his years as a cop to keep his face impassive. As he struggled with his own conflict, it came to him: She *was* scared. Reassuring her would only make her more defensive. Cal scrambled for another approach.

"View it as a business proposition," he said. "If you're seen with me, Mike will think twice before he bothers you again."

Okay, so it was a blatant manipulation of reality. Dana didn't need to know about his run-in with Henderson, which had been more than enough warning for the jerk.

From her viewpoint, this approach just might make sense, even if it struck a killer blow to Cal's ego. He wanted her willing and excited to be with him, but he'd take her whatever way he could get her.

She hesitated. "So this would be kind of a work night for you, and I'd only be going to gain some protection?"

"Sure," he said, swallowing the bitter pill.

"Then I suppose I could do it."

"Great," Cal said, feeling distinctly underwhelmed. "It will be a night to remember."

He just hoped those memories wouldn't crop up in his nightmares.

12

ACTS OF DEFIANCE were something Dana had once practiced frequently. Today she was brushing up on her skills.

"I'm not sure about this," Hallie said as she rinsed Dana's hair in one of the salon's bowls.

"It's no different than the highlights I put in for the last Summer Fun picnic."

"Those had a certain patriotic flair. These are, um…"

"Pink?"

"That would be the word."

Dana had chosen her new hot-pink highlights to stand out against her pale skin. They also clashed gloriously with the electric-blue dress she'd chosen for tonight's Spring Benefit. She couldn't be more in your face without body art. And there she'd drawn the line. She'd never been able to get past the image of what a tattoo would look like on her when she was seventy.

"So do you want to tell me why you're *really* doing this?" Hallie had asked that question in one form or another at least a dozen times this afternoon.

Dana closed her eyes. The full answer would take months on a shrink's couch to unravel.

She knew she was scared to death about going to this dance with Cal. Not only did she think he was committing career suicide, but she wasn't anywhere near prepared to deal with the women on the Spring Benefit committee. Her mother, a mere committee minion, was the warmest of the bunch.

Their clique had never come near Devine Secrets, and never would. Gathering in the crème of Chicago trunk-slammer society was no problem. But the Westshore crew? No way.

Over the past several days, as Dana had dwelled on a plan for dealing with the Spring Benefit, an old quote had played through her mind: *Give the people what they want.*

The Westshore women expected—no, wanted—her to be a wild thing. How else could they bolster their own egos? Besides, no one could hurt her if she bit first.

"Look," Hallie said as Dana's silence stretched out, "I know you're not thrilled about having to go to the benefit, and I know Cal wouldn't be your first choice as a date—"

She could no longer hide the truth from her best friend. "Hallie, there's something you need to know. I saw Cal in Chicago."

"Yeah, he saw you, you two said hi, and—"

"Then we spent the night together in my room."

"No way!" Hallie lost control of the water. It sprayed across Dana's forehead and ran down her face.

"You don't have to drown me," Dana said as her hand closed over the nubby terry cloth towel she'd laid across the arm of the neighboring chair.

Hallie turned the water off and moved around the bowl to take a seat next to Dana, who had sat up and was drying her hair.

"We've been seeing each other since then, too."

"This is fantastic! The first time I saw you two together, I knew you were made for each other!"

"Let's just say we get along better in certain arenas than others." She paused, gathering her thoughts. "I don't want anyone knowing about Cal and me. I never want to feel as though I've hurt his chances to win the permanent appointment as police chief."

"Hurt his chances how?"

"I have a certain...ah, reputation," she said as she finished toweling off her new pink do. "And I'm not just talking about the hair."

Hallie scowled. "Anyone who knows you understands that's ancient history."

"That's the point. Anyone who knows me... Everybody else is perfectly content to go by word of mouth."

"Forget those people."

"I can and you can, but right now, Cal can't."

"Cal cares about you, and there's no way he's going to hide his feelings to protect his job."

"This has been about sex, nothing more."

Hallie snorted. "Cal's a Brewer. Trust me, in the Brewer family nothing happens without hearts being involved, no matter how much we might wish it were otherwise."

"Not this time."

Her friend's smile was unbelievably smug. "If thinking that makes you feel better, be my guest."

SHE SHOULD HAVE GONE with the tattoo.

That night, when Dana opened her front door and

ushered Cal into the living room, he looked appreciative, but not shocked.

"Great dress," he said, his eyes lingering on the skin
exposed by the plunging neckline. "You look gorgeous."

"It's vintage," she replied. "My tribute to Lauren Bacall. Can't you see Bogie's ghost hovering over there in
the corner with Old Lady Pierson?"

"Smart ghost," he said.

Thinking maybe his gaze hadn't traveled above her
cleavage, she raised her fingertips to fluff her spiked
highlights. "Of course, I've updated the Bacall look."

He simply smiled.

Yes, it seemed that the ability to shock diminished in
direct proportion to the number of times one exercised
it. A tattoo of an anaconda coiling up her right arm and
down to her breast might have done the trick, but pink
hair was yesterday's news.

As Mr. V and Olivia cornered Cal and made him
promise not to keep her out too late without calling,
Dana allowed herself to take in how spectacular he
was.

Just about any man could look good in a tuxedo, but
a rare few could make a woman's heart sing. Cal fell
into that group. The white of his shirt set off the dark
tones of his skin, and his eyes seemed even bluer than
usual tonight. It also didn't hurt that he was tall and
most definitely fit.

He caught her checking him out and sent a quick
wink her way. All the while, he assured Olivia that his
intentions were honorable.

Dana gathered her black velvet wrap from the back of Mr. V's orange leather recliner.

"Well, shall we?" she asked, nodding toward the door.

Olivia wasn't quite done. "Didn't you bring her flowers? It's not a Spring Benefit without a corsage. Butterflies are helpful," she added.

Cal reached into the breast pocket of his tuxedo. "I decided to go for something a little different."

He handed Dana a flat, blue velvet jeweler's box. Her hands trembled as she opened it. Once she had, tears began to well.

Inside the box was a delicate gold chain. At intervals on it rested small, gold high-heeled shoes, each a different style, but all twinkling with tiny diamonds.

Nobody had ever given her something this wonderful before. In fact, her wedding ring from Mike had been of the gumball-machine variety.

Speechless, she looked up at Cal.

His smile was tentative, almost as though he'd been worried about whether she'd like his gift. Seeing his concern touched her all the more.

"I'd kind of noticed you have a thing for shoes," he said.

She wondered whether he'd also noticed she had a thing for him.

"It's beautiful. Could you help me put it on?" Issuing a silent thank-you to the inventor of waterproof mascara, she subtly wiped the tears rimming her eyes.

Cal took the box and freed the necklace. When he stepped behind her, she tipped her head down so he could latch the fine chain. He lingered long enough to press a kiss on the back of her neck and whisper "perfect" to her.

Dana sighed. She closed her eyes and savored the moment. Maybe she could have skipped the pink highlights and the tattoo.

CAL STEELED HIMSELF to run the gauntlet of committee members stationed just inside the country club's front door. As he took Dana's left hand and rested it over the inside of his right arm, he noticed her fingers were far chillier than the cool night air could have caused. She was also dragging her feet in a very un-Dana-like way.

"We'll make it fast," he promised, nodding toward the committee. "Two words to each of them."

"'Get stuffed'?" she suggested.

He bit back a smile. "I was thinking more in terms of 'great decorations.'"

"Spoilsport."

"Let's just do it and then find Steve and Hallie."

"Sounds like a plan."

Cal hid a wince. When faced with this night, no doubt Dana had concocted a plan, two backups and a contingency. He'd known she'd worked herself into a state when he'd seen the pink hair. Maybe she'd intended to knock everyone off balance with the statement, but he liked the highlights.

Really.

He smiled at her. Slivers of green shone in her hazel eyes.

"Race you to the champagne," she said as they joined the receiving line.

Their chorus of "great decorations" continued unbroken until they landed in front of the last committee member. He felt Dana's hand tense where it rested against his tuxedo jacket.

"Mother," she said in a subdued voice. "You look lovely."

Cal had seen happier faces on guys he'd just taken down and cuffed than the one Mrs. Devine wore. Through his years as a police officer, he'd learned that some people simply needed extra guidance before they behaved. He'd lay odds that she was one of those folks.

"I think the Devine women are the most beautiful here tonight," he interrupted before Dana's mother could speak. He brushed a kiss against Dana's cheek. "Then again, I'm biased."

Mrs. Devine's mouth opened once, twice, but she said nothing. She compressed it into a thin line and glared at Dana's hair. Finally, a very grudging "thank you" worked free of her lips.

As they walked away, Dana squeezed his arm and murmured, "My hero."

He liked the sound of that.

CHAMPAGNE AND MUSIC had a way of making even the most uncomfortable evening more tolerable. Cal Brewer had a way of making it downright magical.

Everyone seemed to be in a welcoming mood when Cal was around. During dinner, even her mother and her friends had stopped by to talk about having a ladies' day once the day spa was open. About the only one who hadn't let his guard down was Richard MacNee, but he was politically astute enough to work the crowd on the other side of the ballroom.

She and Cal danced, laughed, talked and then danced some more. Just after ten, he left her with Steve and Hallie while he had a quick word with the mayor. Dana was happy for the break. Her mock alligator pumps had been a case of brief infatuation. If she had walked more than five steps in them, she would have never bought them. Her toes were pinched, and she thought she could feel a blister starting on her left heel.

The band struck up a new tune. Steve and Hallie gave each other that "they're playing our song" look.

"Go on, you two," Dana said, shooing them in the direction of the dance floor. "I'm a big girl. I promise I can stand here all by myself."

"If you're sure..." Hallie said with the proper degree of best friend hesitation, but she already had Steve by the hand and was on her way.

Warm from the press of bodies and the time spent dancing, Dana looked longingly out the French doors to the back terrace. After a moment, she gave up on acting like she was thrilled to be standing there sweaty and alone, and slipped outside.

The night was clear and warm for mid-May. Crickets sang with the muted music drifting from the club-house.

Smiling, Dana strolled to the edge of the terrace. Resting one hand on the stone balustrade that marked its border, she slipped off first one shoe, then the other.

"Much better," she said with a sigh. She knew she'd pay when it was time to put them back on, but for now, comfort ruled.

"You never could keep your shoes on after a night of partying," a voice said from behind her.

Dana gripped the rail tighter. "I didn't see you here, Mike."

He stood next to her, now. "I saw you...couldn't miss you."

Even in the dim glow cast by the club's lighting, he looked tired, almost worn around the edges.

"I need to talk to you," he said.

Thinking ahead, she began to slip her right foot back inside its shoe. "Just for a second. I promised Cal I'd be back."

She could hear the band winding down for a break, and the sets of doors onto the broad terrace open as more party-goers stepped outside to admire the starlit night.

"I'm kind of in a situation," Mike said. "I might be leaving town for a while—just until things cool down."

Right shoe on, Dana lined up her left shoe with the tip of her foot. The shoe wobbled, then fell over. Seeing no way out, she bent to straighten it and wedge her poor foot back in. When she stood, he gripped her upper arms.

"I want you to come with me."

She couldn't have heard him properly. "You what?"

"Florida, maybe."

She tried to step back, but couldn't. Unsettled, she shot the first flip comment that came to mind. "Too much sunshine."

"Come on, Dana. Game's up." He pulled her against him. He smelled of stale beer. She turned her head away. "You've made your point with Cal Brewer. You made me suffer, and now it's time to come home."

His fingers pressed into the side of her face as he

forced her to turn back to him. Before she could even draw a breath, his mouth slammed over hers.

Instinct could be a harsh guide. Hard and fast, Dana slugged him in the stomach. Mike doubled over and gasped a word not often heard on the Westshore Country Club's genteel terrace.

Victorious, she swiped her hand across her mouth. What she'd give for some sort of antibacterial wipe.

"Let's get this straight," she said after taking a few quick steps out of his potential reach. "Cal's the best thing that's ever happened to me. He's smart and honest and hardworking, and he's kinder to me than any man has been. You, on the other hand, should be counting yourself lucky not to be in jail yet. Go to Florida, Mike, and don't come back."

She swung toward the ballroom, then stopped as she saw the crowd that had gathered between her and the doors.

"Dandy." She figured she could either brazen it out or act like a wilting flower. Brazen suited her better.

"Someone might want to get him a glass of water," she said to the spectators. "Then again, maybe not."

Cal was at her side before she could even wonder how he got there. He wrapped his arm around her and walked with her to the clubhouse. "The best thing ever, huh?"

For once, Dana chose silence.

THEY DROVE AWAY from Westshore without talking, Cal because he was busy reveling in what he'd heard Dana say, and Dana probably because she was in shock.

He'd just pulled off the highway when she finally seemed to notice her surroundings. "Where are you taking me?"

"Home," he said.

"Then you turned off three miles early."

"My home."

"Oh."

A few minutes later they pulled up in front of the farmhouse. The porch lights on either side of the front door shone like beacons to Cal's future. He smiled. Everything was so clear now.

He switched off the engine, then went around to open Dana's door.

"Thanks," she murmured as he helped her from the Explorer.

He'd never even considered bringing another woman here for the night, but this just felt...*right*. She stood in the living room, looking so overwhelmed that he had to kiss her, so he did. Once and with all the tenderness he felt for this tough girl with a heart so big she didn't begin to know how to handle it.

"This place is wonderful, Cal. It's warm and happy—a real home."

He lifted the velvet wrap from her shoulders and draped it over the back of a chair. "I want you to spend the night with me tonight. Here."

"But Mitch will be home sooner or later, and—"

He smiled. "Sweetheart, Mitch knew about us before I had it figured out."

She looked so puzzled that he knew she hadn't gotten there yet herself. He also knew that she'd have to work this out on her own, and in her own time. That was one of the things he loved most about her. There was no leading Dana Devine anywhere she didn't choose to go.

He held out his hand to her. "Will you come upstairs with me, now?"

She hesitated, and Cal's heart seemed to suspend between beats. Nothing in his life had ever mattered so much.

Then she placed her hand in his.

Cal smiled as his life reshaped itself into something marvelous and exciting. He could wait, he thought as he led her up the broad oak stairs.

He could wait to tell her that for every night as long as they lived, he wanted to lead her up this staircase and make love to her.

He could wait, but not much longer.

13

DANA WOKE to the music of birds singing, more birds than she ever heard in town. Their songs were joyous, demanding, all the things Cal had been with her last night. She stayed snuggled on her stomach with her eyes closed, not yet ready to admit that morning had arrived. Seeking Cal, she reached out one hand, but found she was alone in their warm nest of flannel sheets.

"Good morning," she heard him say.

She opened her eyes, rolled onto her back and returned his greeting. "Good morning."

He had already showered and dressed. In one hand he held her dress. His other hand was behind his back.

"Sleep well?" he asked.

There was something so intimate about his smile. That same something had been there when they made love last night.

Love.

Dana drew in a slow breath as the world around her grew brighter.

Love. She'd never felt it before. Not like this, anyway, which was the only excuse she could come up with for not accepting it sooner.

"I found your dress, but I can't seem to find anything that went under it, other than these." He brought his other hand around and held up two sheer, thigh-high black stockings with their matching lace garters.

"That's because there wasn't anything much."

His eyebrows rose. "You mean I got you undressed last night and somehow missed that?"

Dana laughed. "You must have been distracted," she said as she drew back the covers.

Cal's answering smile was slow and sexy.

"You have a way of doing that to me." He draped the long dress over the bed's carved wooden footboard and dropped the stockings back on the floor. As he looked at her, she knew he wanted her, but it was there again, that special spark...that love.

He climbed back into bed, and she twined her arms around his neck and kissed him with the love she felt, but still feared to voice.

"I don't know what you're going to wear down to breakfast," he said while caressing the line of her jaw with his thumbs. "That is, assuming we're left with the strength to eat."

Dana did her best to make sure they were good and tired.

ONCE MORNING had officially arrived, they decided that the underwear issue was unresolvable. After they showered together, Dana ended up going downstairs in one of Cal's T-shirts, which was almost as long as a dress on her. Over that, she wore a bathrobe she was willing to bet had hung in his closet since he'd received it as a gift from a distant relative. Anyone who knew him could see that Cal wasn't a bathrobe kind of man. Dana busied herself with the coffeemaker so she didn't have to deal with Mitch, who was sitting at the kitchen table grinning like a fool.

"Something funny?" she heard Cal ask his brother.

"Can't a guy just be happy?" Mitch asked.

"Why don't you go be happy on the job?"

"Not even a cup of coffee?"

Cal slapped a couple of dollars down on the table. "My treat. Now get lost, you're making Dana edgy."

On his way out the door, Mitch stopped long enough to plant a kiss on Dana's cheek. "See you, Sis," he said.

Sis?

She shot a confused look Cal's way, but he seemed suddenly enthralled by something in the fridge. Maybe Brewers were just squirrelly in the morning.

The phone rang. Cal picked it up while muttering something about Hallie being the next to gloat. "Hello?"

He looked kind of surprised by whoever was on the other end. After a long silence, he said, "I'll let her know, and I promise it won't happen again."

After he hung up, he came and wrapped his arms around Dana. She leaned into his strength, loving the way they fit together so perfectly.

"That was Olivia Hawkins and Mr. V," he said. "They wanted you to know that if you stay out all night, you're expected to call home."

Dana smiled.

"And Olivia wants you to help her pick out a wedding dress."

"Really?"

Cal laughed, but she didn't blame him. She'd squealed like teenager being asked to the prom.

"How utterly cool," she said with more maturity...but not much. Life could get no better than this.

CAL DROPPED DANA at home and then decided to put in a few hours at the station catching up on paperwork and preparing for his final interview with the town council. He hadn't been working more than an hour when the phone rang.

In response to his greeting he got, "Mike Henderson has messed with my life for the very last time."

This time, Cal knew it was Dana. He also knew he was far too involved in her life to do his job properly. In fact, he needed the whole matter moved out of his control—both direct and indirect. He didn't want to have the opportunity to wrap his hands around Henderson's neck. After calling over to the county sheriff's office for someone to meet him, he took off for Devine Secrets. He was barely inside the front door before Dana gripped him by the wrist and hauled him around to the back side of the reception desk.

"Look at this!" She pointed to a pile of ashes, melted plastic and one spiral wire on the floor.

"I'm looking. What is it?"

"My appointment book."

After the scissors incident, Cal knew there was more mystery to what made a salon tick than a guy could grasp. He tread carefully, not wanting to upset her further.

"Everything in the appointment book is on the computer, right?" He phrased it as a question, but he hoped like hell it was a statement.

"Um...not exactly."

"How much less than exactly?"

She used the back of her hand to wipe a tear from her face. The sight ate at Cal's heart.

"Like one-hundred percent less," she said. "The computer died a couple of months ago. I meant to get a new one, but money kept getting tighter and tighter, and then I just kind of forgot about it."

Cal scrambled to grab hold of a reassuring thought. "At least he didn't burn down the salon."

Another tear trekked down her cheek. "Lucky me. My life was in that book. It's going to take me days to reconstruct my schedule, and I can't leave the salon during open hours until I do."

Jim Caldwell, one of Cal's buddies from the sheriff's office, arrived. Cal sat next to Dana and held her hand as she told Jim about arriving at the salon and finding the back door jimmied open. Cal tried to keep out of the conversation and succeeded until the very end. He took Jim aside and told him the first place to go was to Mike Henderson's. Odds were he wouldn't have to go much farther.

After Jim left, Cal asked Dana, "Do you have anything scheduled for this afternoon?"

"No, other than some wailing and gnashing of the teeth, I'm fresh out of plans."

"No plans? That's the first good news I've heard since I got here."

"Funny."

Except he wasn't joking. He wanted to see her secure enough that she didn't feel compelled to plot and plan for decades in advance. "Here's what we're doing.

We're going to Muskegon. First stop is to buy you a new computer—"

"But I—"

"After that, we're picking up new locks and keys and a steel door for the back of this place. And tomorrow I'm calling someone to have a full security system installed."

Her hazel eyes narrowed. "I don't want a security system. What's the benefit of living in a small town if I have to lock up like it's the big city? Besides, I refuse to be a coward."

"There's one helluva difference between being a coward and showing some common sense."

"A stronger door is common sense. The rest is—"

Part of Cal was pleased that she was feeling good enough to argue. The rest of him was fighting hard not to lose patience. "If you argue with me about this, I'm going to haul you back to the station and stick you in protective custody, got it?"

She frowned. "Nice sentiment, but technically, I'm not sure you can do that."

Cal looked heavenward for guidance, but all he saw was some cherub his sister had painted on the ceiling smirking down at him. He glared at Dana, who clearly had her attitude set in "I can do it myself" mode.

He blurted the first thing that came to mind. "I love you, dammit, but you're making me crazy."

She didn't have much to say after that. Then again, neither did he.

MIKE HAD DISAPPEARED. Dana couldn't decide whether she should be relieved that he was gone or worried that he was probably hiding while he planned another way to throw her life into turmoil.

The personal protection order that Cal had prodded her into getting didn't make her feel much better. Mike didn't seem to have a whole lot of respect for paper, and that's all it was.

In the week since her planner had been reduced to ash, she had been trapped in the salon. She had reconstructed her schedule the best she could, based on her standing appointments and Trish's planner, but there were too many gaps.

The only redeeming event was having a new computer. With her Internet connection back, she filled those times when maybe she had a client coming in, but maybe not, with cyber shoe shopping.

Cal came by daily, and they spent every night out at the farm. But for all those hours together, he hadn't said another word about loving her. She really needed a declaration of love not given under duress—and without either a *dammit* or a *crazy* included—before she was going to feel safe in admitting her feelings.

So as she waited, Dana shopped with an eye to remaking herself into a woman who could stand by a police chief's side without driving him crazy. She bought quiet shoes...elegant shoes... Well, to her eyes, they were boring shoes, but they fit this new image she was sculpting. She also stripped the hot pink highlights out of her hair. Cal said he missed them, but she figured he was just being nice. She had been a tad depressed lately. Being a girl without a plan—or a planner— didn't suit her any better than her new shoes.

This evening, in an effort to cheer her up, Hallie had

come over to the salon to help her paint two small occasional tables in a tiger theme for the Eden Room. One table was finished when they had run out of the deep orange hue.

While Hallie ran back to her studio for more supplies, Dana had been amusing herself by painting names beneath various animals on the walls with a fine-haired brush. Cal was a lion, Hallie an antelope and Mike the snake, of course.

She'd just started naming a flame-feathered parrot after Trish when she heard the front door chime.

"That was fast," she murmured. By the time she finished the *h* in Trish, Hallie still hadn't appeared.

"No fair taking a break without me," she called, but no one answered. Fair was fair. Dana set aside her paintbrush, wiped her hands on the legs of her already paint-covered jeans, and walked toward the salon's front room.

"So did you pick up some chocolate? Hiding the good stuff on me?" she joked.

Dana stopped in the doorway. Hallie hadn't come in, but Mike had. He stood in front of her styling station, handling one of her pairs of scissors.

"What are you doing here?" she asked, trying to keep her voice level.

He shrugged. "Checking things out." He put the scissors down.

So much for court orders. "You need to leave."

He sat instead, then propped his feet on the countertop in front of him. Dana watched his face in the mirror. He'd switched off the charm. His eyes were dead cold.

"You made a fool of me last week."

"You did that for yourself," she shot back, then immediately regretted it. She tried for a conciliatory tone. "Mike, I don't see any point in discussing this."

"Do you love him?"

Dana didn't pretend to misunderstand. "Yes."

He stood, then swept his arm across the counter, sending cans and bottles flying. He was unsteady on his feet—not staggering, but not on an even keel, either.

Dana knew she was in far over her head. She glanced toward the telephone. He followed the motion of her eyes. In three long steps he reached the phone and ripped the cord from the wall jack. "Think I'm going to make this easy on you after you trashed me in front of everyone who counts?"

Now she was really scared.

"I'm tired of working this hard. You were supposed to need me. You were supposed to come crawling back," he shouted.

He kicked over the manicure cart. The glass tray on the top shattered. Nail polish bottles rolled across the floor.

How could she have ever thought she loved this man? Week by week, piece by piece, he had been working to destroy everything she'd fought to build. Dana didn't pause to think. If she had, she wouldn't have launched herself at his back. They both landed on the floor, sending one of the two reception chairs skidding into the front door.

Ignoring the pain shooting through her left knee, she

dragged in a breath. "How could you?" she cried. "How could you ruin my life like this?"

Mike was already on his feet. He kicked the small magazine table. It shot past Dana and slammed into the chair. He yanked her upright. Hands gripping her shirt, he emphasized each of his words with a shake. "You threw me out."

She pulled backward, trying to free herself. "You were sleeping with another woman!" Dana locked her hands over his. "Just let me go."

"Not until you listen."

She bit his arm. Hard.

He shoved her back to the floor. Dana pushed herself toward the door, looking for a quick escape, wondering where the hell Hallie was. Before she had a chance to get any closer, Mike grabbed her by the wrist and dragged her in front of the mirror.

"Look at us. We're perfect together. Perfect!"

Dana stared at their reflection. She looked furious, an appearance in stark contrast to reality. She was more terrified than she'd ever been.

Mike was a total stranger, not even a whisper of the party guy she'd married. He was gripped by something she couldn't begin to understand.

Dana recounted the facts slowly, carefully. "Mike, you slept with Suzanne. We got divorced. We'll never be together."

He dug his fingers into her shoulders so hard she had to fight to hide her wince of pain.

"Don't you get it?" His voice was even louder now, maybe enough that someone would hear, she prayed. "She was just another mark. It didn't mean anything."

The words were sharper than a blow. "A mark? Is that what I was, too?"

He snorted. "You don't have nearly enough money. You're more of an addiction."

Dana thought back to those days in Chicago, especially those when Mike had said he was going to show up, but never did.

"She wasn't the first time you cheated on me," she said flatly.

"None of them meant anything. You're the only woman I've ever loved."

"Let go," she said in as level a voice as she could pull together. "You're hurting me."

Mike took a step back. "I've wasted weeks trying to make you see how much you need me. I'm the only one who can give you what you want."

"I think you mean I'm the only one who was blind enough to cater to you."

"No!" He picked up the stool she sat on while trimming hair and flung it at the mirror. The metal casters on the bottom of the stool hit like hammers. Dana instinctively ducked her head as the glass flew. Still, tiny shards cut into her.

"You love me!" He was beyond reasoning, beyond anything Dana had ever dealt with.

She started to scream, and when she did, she chose the one word that might gain a passerby's attention: "*Fire!*"

Over and over she shouted as Mike fought to clamp his hand over her mouth.

He pinned her to the floor in the middle of the glass

and brushes and hair products. Dana knew this was now about survival.

"We'll leave," he said. "Don't you see this is the way it has to be? We'll move someplace else, start again...."

Dana thought maybe she heard a siren in the distance. She kept fighting. Damned if she'd go down any other way. Her hand closed over a can.

Please don't let it be mousse.

She inched her fingers forward and felt the small pump button of hairspray.

Yes!

She dragged the can toward her, gripped it and took aim for his eyes. When he let go of her to grab his face, she planted her knee where he most deserved it.

His howl came at the same time as the sound of snapping wood and shattering glass. A deep voice—one she loved to the bottom of her soul—shouted, "Police! Don't move."

Mike was too busy writhing on the floor to listen. Dana rolled to her knees and pulled herself to her feet.

She touched her fingers to her forehead. They came away red with blood.

"Dana?"

Hallie ran to her side. "I heard the noise from the top of the stairs and called the police...ah, Cal. The door was jammed with something and I couldn't get in," she said while pulling off her sweatshirt. She pressed the cuff of one sleeve to Dana's forehead.

Dana yelped. "Watch it, that hurts!"

"I think it's just a little nick, but those scalp wounds like to bleed," Hallie said without letting up the pressure.

"Should I call an ambulance?" asked another voice.

"Would somebody shut Henderson up? Got a gag on you, Chief?" a third voice called to Cal.

Dana pushed enough of the sweatshirt out of her face to see that a crowd had come down the steps and gathered in the entry of the salon. Anna, the bartender from Truro's, stood next to them with about half of the tavern's regulars behind her. Though she couldn't see him, she thought she heard Mayor Talbert's booming voice.

"Is anyone not here?" she muttered to Hallie.

"Sandy Bend at its finest," was her friend's philosophical answer. "Now sit down before you faint."

"Only sissies faint," Dana answered, but settled in the styling chair as directed. She was seeing some pretty interesting shooting stars, not that she'd ever admit it.

She wiped something slick from her cheek. Damn Mike. It smelled like her favorite rosemary-infused, fifteen-bucks-a-jar hair pomade. Feeling marginally better, she began to take stock of the damage to her salon. Tonight's battle made the first break-in look like the amateur night it had been.

"Missy Guyer's going to have a fit. I'd better start coming up with a new insurance plan," she murmured.

"You can probably hang on for an hour or two before coming up with a plan," Hallie said.

Her friend had a point.

Dana saw that Cal had handcuffed Mike and hauled him to his feet. Cal's mouth was drawn into a tight, angry line.

"What are you all staring at?" Mike snarled to the crowd. Cal hitched him tighter under his elbow, but Mike kept going. "I dumped her again and she's got a temper, okay?"

"Shut up." Cal's voice was low and threatening.

"Can't take the truth? You think you're the only one who's had Dana in his bed lately? You've been sharing, Chief, and you didn't even know it."

Cal clamped one broad hand on the back of Mike's neck and shoved him through the crowd and out the door.

In his wake there was nothing but silence.

Dana ducked her face into Hallie's sweatshirt and waited for the world to go away. She had spent a lifetime telling herself and anyone who would listen that she didn't care about what others thought. That she was tougher than rumor and gossip.

It had been a lie.

The pain was so wrenching she couldn't breathe. Cal Brewer was lost to her, and Dana didn't care to go on.

14

With morning came clarity. Dana knew what she had to do. In some bizarre way, her mother had been right. She couldn't continue to let the insanity of her life poison Cal's.

His future was to be decided by the town council this afternoon. Dana suspected that future would be less murky if she removed herself from it.

She pushed through the police station door before she lost her nerve. Cal was on the phone. He nodded a quick greeting in her direction, and Dana looked away before the tears could start. Her stomach sunk as she noticed Mitch and Jim Caldwell, the county deputy she'd met when Mike burned her appointment book. She hadn't been prepared for a public breakup, especially not after last night. To make matters worse, Mitch was headed her way.

"Hey," he said, then pressed a quick kiss on her cheek. "Are you doing okay this morning?"

Because she knew words would give away her heartbreak, Dana simply nodded.

"Mike's been transferred over to the county jail," he said. "I'm willing to bet no one will post bond for him, so you should be rid of him until the trial."

"Good," she managed to whisper.

Cal finished up his phone call and came to stand by his brother.

"Is there someplace we can talk?" Dana asked.

He glanced around and then said, "Would you guys mind giving us a minute alone?"

Mitch and Jim stepped out the front door.

Cal brushed back her hair to check the nick on her forehead. "Looks like you won't have a scar," he said.

At least, not one that showed, Dana thought.

She drew in a breath. "I don't want to see you anymore."

"What do you mean?"

"It's not working...it's not what I had expected." Those words held a world of truth. She hadn't expected to fall in love with him. She hadn't expected to find that a man in so many ways different from her could also be her soulmate.

"Just when did you decide this?"

"I've—I've been thinking about it for a while." She pulled together the shreds of her tough chick persona. "You knew this wasn't serious between us, Cal, so don't bother getting angry. You're better off this way."

She couldn't look at him anymore, not without breaking down and crying. "I'll see you around," she said and bolted for the door.

"*YOU'RE BETTER OFF THIS WAY.*"

Cal leaned back in his chair and shook his head. She'd actually expected him to fall for that load of manure. Of course, not so many months ago, he had back in Chicago. The difference was that time when she'd run, she'd been scared. This time she was being crazy.

Comforted by one saving thought, he grinned at the ceiling. She'd been wearing the necklace he'd given her, and he knew that when Dana booted someone from her life, she did it totally. That necklace was just where it belonged, and soon, he would be, too.

His complacency was short-lived. Cal sat up as a horrible realization came to him. This was Dana, a woman who was a virtuoso in stubbornness. If she decided she was dumping him, he could consider himself dumped.

"It's not happening, sweetheart," he said, though he knew she was well down the street and probably busy coming up with one-year and five-year plans to avoid him.

Cal knew it would take something major to show Dana that he couldn't be scared off. Something public. Steve told Hallie he loved her in the middle of the Summer Fun parade, but no way was Cal waiting for the parade to come around again.

He'd just have to make his own spectacle... something big enough to let every citizen of Sandy Bend know that he loved Dana Devine, and if that bothered them, they could adjust to life with Big Brother MacNee at the helm of the police force.

Cal picked up the phone and dialed the number of someone he knew was very talented at creating a spectacle. "Hey, Hal," he said. "Do you have some time you can spare me?"

DANA LAY on the chaise in Trish's room with a cold, damp towel over her eyes, which, after the failure of cucumber slices and tea bags, was a final resort in the fight to bring down the puffiness. As she lay there listening to calming New Age music, and feeling no calmer for it, she heard the bells on the front door chime. Then chime a few more times.

She refused to be curious. Curious meant she cared what was going on in that awful world out there. And she didn't. Not one bit.

The bells rang again.

"Dana, you'd better come here," Trish called.

"Don't want to," she muttered.

Dana heard someone enter the room and then close the door. "Trish, whatever it is—"

The damp towel was whisked from her face.

"You look awful," Hallie said.

Dana gave her friend a deadpan stare. "Gee, I wonder why."

"This won't do," Halle said. She went back to the door, opened it a crack and called. "Trish, get in here. We need a little emergency repair."

Dana closed her eyes. Didn't they know she was beyond repair?

Hallie corralled her over to Trish's table and mirror. "Just sit on the stool and be good."

They applied makeup with such speed that Dana thought Trish might have missed her calling. She belonged on a pit crew at the Brickyard down in Indy.

The two women hovered over Dana, fussing and primping. Dana rolled her eyes and gave a bored sigh.

She would *not* be curious.

"Okay, much better," Hallie said in a satisfied voice. "Now, come on." She wrapped her hand around Dana's wrist and led her to the door.

When it opened, Dana tried to take a hasty step backward. "No way!" Trish shoved her out.

In an eerie echo of last night's disaster, half the town had somehow packed itself into her reception area. Though she was too dazed to take inventory, Dana was pretty sure she saw Mitch, Steve and the mayor. She definitely saw MacNee looking ticked off. Next to him, Olivia and Mr. V were holding hands and smiling at her as if they knew a big secret. And her mother! Dana couldn't begin to imagine what would move her mother to come through the salon's front door. Unless it was to comment on the plywood over the broken glass.

"Okay, what gives?" she asked.

Hallie nudged her side. "Over there."

Dana looked in the direction Hallie was smiling.

Cal sat in her styling chair.

She blinked.

Blinked again.

This was a Cal quite unlike any Cal she'd ever seen.

She moved a couple of steps closer.

No, she definitely wasn't seeing things. His gaze met hers in the mirror and he smiled. He swung the chair around, stood and walked to her.

Dana's shock had receded enough for her to find her voice. "Um...I don't know if you happened to notice this but your hair is—"

"Blue?" he replied in the most casual of voices. "Yeah, I had noticed. It took Hallie the better part of two hours to get it this color."

Dana shot her friend an alarmed look. "Do I want to ask what you used to do this?"

Hallie grinned. "Probably not."

"Okay." Trying to ignore the crowd watching her, Dana paced in a tight circle. "So all of this is supposed to mean what?"

"What it means is that I've called a town meeting. We need to get some things straight around here, the first of which is that I love you. Now, I figure that's usually a pretty personal thing, except apparently in Sandy Bend." He paused to press a kiss against her cheek, and then addressed the crowd watching them with rapt interest. "And since most of you seem to feel you have a stake in who I love, I asked you here."

He went to stand in front of Mayor Talbert and the town council. "You might note that not only am I here taking care of personal business during work hours, but I've effectively trashed the department's grooming policy."

They nodded, some looking righteous and superior, but most looking amused.

"I wanted to make it easy for you to go ahead and give the police chief's job to MacNee, here, if you're so wrapped up in how a man looks or who he gives his heart to. Of course, if you give a damn about how the job is done, you'll give it to me, because I can do it better than anyone else.

"What you see is what you get...well, except the blue hair, if we can figure how to get the spray paint out."

"Spray paint," Dana blurted. "Hallie Brewer Whitman, how could you?"

Cal laughed. "Yell at her later, sweetheart."

He walked to Mr. V. "In a short time you've become a surrogate father...grandfather...hell, I don't quite know what. All I know is that Dana values your opinion. I've already talked to her mother, and now I'd like your permission to ask for Dana's hand in marriage."

Mr. V stood as proud as the flamingoes on his shirt. "You'd better marry her, or—"

He looked ready to issue a threat, but Olivia elbowed him and gave him a stern look. "Or you're just plain nuts," he decreed.

Dana smiled through the tears she could feel messing up Trish's repair job.

Cal stood before her and took her hands in his. "You love me, right?"

The time for playing coy was long past, if it had ever existed at all.

"With all my heart," she said.

"Please marry me, Dana."

Dana Devine recognized her destiny, even when he wore blue hair.

"Of course," she whispered, awed that this moment had arrived.

And as she kissed Cal, the most marvelous wedding plans started dancing in her mind....

A "Mother of the Year" contest brings
overwhelming response as thousands of women
vie for the luxurious grand prize....

Kate Hoffmann

Jacqueline Diamond

Jill Shalvis

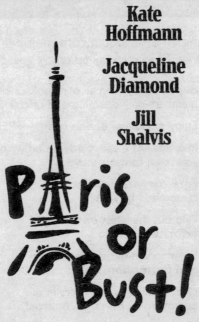

Paris or Bust!

A hilarious and romantic trio of new stories!

With a trip to Paris at stake, these women are
determined to win! But the laughs are many as three of
them discover that being finalists isn't the most
excitement they'll ever have.... Falling in love is!

Available in April 2003.

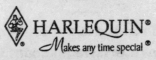

HARLEQUIN®
Makes any time special ®

If you enjoyed what you just read,
then we've got an offer you can't resist!

Take 2 bestselling
love stories FREE!

Plus get a FREE surprise gift!

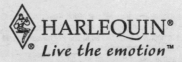

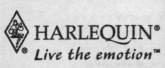

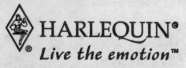

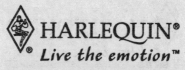

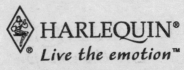